For Jean

Who migrated to my heart one winter night and made it perpetual

summer. More or less.

CREAKWING'S CROSSING

By Peter Harrison

This is a story about the mystery of migration. Many of the events it describes happen every year. The others happened only once. But in that year the mystery was even stranger.

About the author

Peter Harrison began his career on British newspapers and then moved to the BBC working out of Manchester as a reporter for radio and television. After a lifetime in journalism, dealing in facts, he took early retirement to concentrate on fantasy.

He has had stories, talks and plays broadcast on BBC radio, and writes also for the highly acclaimed local theatre, the Garrick, situated in the small town of Altrincham, to the south of Manchester.

The idea for Creakwing's Crossing came to him from the experience of awakening on mornings in September to discover the swallows had gone — and wondering how they were faring.

This book is also available in e-book format from
www.authorsonline.co.uk

An AuthorsOnLine Book

Published by Authors OnLine Ltd 2002

ISBN 0 7552 0063 2

Authors OnLine Ltd
40 Castle Street
Hertford SG14 1HR
England

Visit us online at <u>www.authorsonline.co.uk</u>

Long Before

Since the beginning of time we have shared the world with the swallows, close enough to be able to hear the faint sound of their squeaky cry and sometimes so close that it has been possible to see that in appearance they are not dark and ordinary at all but brightly and mysteriously coloured.

What is not generally known, however, is that all this time the swallows have also been observing us and listening to the sound of our voices. Through the centuries certain names have come floating up to the swallows in the still of the day and the quiet of the night. The names of those who have come to be renowned among men for great and stirring deeds.

That was how the custom came to be established among the swallows of using the names they heard most often to honour those among their own number who had also gained fame and renown and deserved to be remembered.

From one generation to another most of the swallows would forget, if indeed they ever knew, why these names had once been famous among humans but in each generation one swallow was appointed to be the Keeper of the Names, to ensure that they were faithfully remembered and passed down.

Sometimes, many years would go by without the need for a name to be bestowed but always they would be whispered on from one century to the next until the time came for one of them to be proclaimed.

It happened sometimes, in spite of the Keeper's most faithful efforts, that a name became so dimly remembered that there would come a day when the whisper of the name was lost on the wind and no one knew that it had gone but always there were new names to take their place.

Most of the swallows never had a name at all and even those who did win the right to bear a name were given it after the exploit and not before, for obvious reasons.

Our story tells of the way in which no fewer than six swallows achieved this honour in the space of a single migration and to make the events easier to follow I have taken the liberty of using throughout the "fame names" which were given to them much later when the full story of the Winter Crossing became known.

Chapter 1

On summer mornings, long before it was light, the whole forest would come noisily to life again as the birds who lived there greeted the new day in the swelling anthem of the dawn chorus, with the exception, that is, of Wake[1] who preferred to remain in bed.

Ever since he could remember (which of course was not very long) Wake had found the idea of the dawn chorus very hard to understand. In the first place he considered it a most unreasonable time to wake up, but the idea of waking up in the dark and simultaneously bursting into song irritated him immensely. To tell the truth he was not alone in this prejudice. It was well-known that many other animals living in the forest, including quite a few birds, claimed to suffer with their nerves because of the dawn chorus. That morning, as he lay in his nest, trying in vain to cover his ears with his feathers, the noise seemed even louder than usual.

"You can't even see," Wake grumbled to his mother who was listening admiringly to the concert from her perch near the door of the barn. It really was surprising to see how musical she had become ever since three of his brothers and sisters had been admitted to the swallow section.

"Waking people up," he continued when he detected no response from his mother.

"Oh, do be quiet," she said serenely. "You know it's the tradition."

"But what about before?" Wake persisted, in the entirely reasonable voice which he had noticed with pleasure did seem to have the power to irritate older birds. "It wasn't traditional before someone started it. One morning did someone just say: 'I suppose we ought to have a tradition of waking people up in the mornings before it's light, by singing to them for an hour and then stopping, so that everyone is wide awake with nothing to do until the sun comes up?"

---

[1] *Those who maintain that swallows have no real sense of humour should reflect on the satirical quality of the "fame name" selected for Wake during the often uproarious naming council which followed long after the Crossing.*

1

"Pardon? " pleaded his mother, vaguely.

"I said"-----

"Oh, do shut up," said his mother. "Just because you don't want to get up in the mornings you want to spoil it for those who do. Anyway you know why we have the dawn chorus. It's the way that all the birds of the forest greet the new day."

"It's the way that all the birds of the forest look for a fight, more likely," said Wake.[2]

All at once, with what appeared to be a considerable effort of will, his mother looked at him with interest for the first time that morning.

"Anyway you're right for once," she remarked affectionately. "It is a little bit earlier this morning. It's because everyone is so excited."

Wake knew immediately what she meant. For him it had been a wonderful year so far. It had all begun with him being born earlier in the summer. He was not quite clear what he had been doing before that but he was absolutely convinced that being alive was preferable.

In just a few short months he had learned many new skills. He had learned how to argue; how to disobey instructions; and even on occasions how to be less than polite to his dear mother. Not bad going, he considered, for a swallow in his very first year. And now it was all about to culminate in the great adventure of the Crossing. That was what the excitement was all about. And the anxiety, too, for it had been impossible not to notice the way the older birds had suddenly started to take a deep interest in the younger ones like himself who would be making the Crossing for the very first time.

All the young swallows considered their flying skills to be just about perfect, especially when they compared them with some of the techniques they had observed in other birds and yet their parents, who had given every indication of being lost in admiration earlier in the summer, now seemed most uneasy. Every day now the young swallows were being ordered to practise flying farther and farther away from the barn.

---

[2] *In making this observation Wake was betraying a wisdom which belied his tender months, for it is a fact that first thing in the morning some birds do sing rather belligerently.*

And when they were not practising flying they were practising eating! Or at least that was how it seemed to them. Even when they were completely full and politely protested that they really could not manage even so much as a small fly their parents continued to press food upon them, accompanied by an instruction which, it must be said, found no disfavour with certain greedy, young swallows who had already been following the recommended course privately. "You must put some weight on for the Crossing," was a most agreeable instruction, so far as they were concerned.

The Crossing; he just wished he could understand why all those swallows who had made the journey politely declined to discuss the matter, including his mother. Whenever he pressed her to tell him what was going to happen she would lose patience and cuff his ear and then press him remorsefully to her bosom until he blushed with shame.

That morning, however, he could tell from her manner that the time had almost come for the journey to begin. And still he knew practically nothing about what was to happen. Perhaps, he reflected. he could find the answer to his questions down at the pond.

The pond, a vast, wind-ruffled pool, so wide that he had only once flown to the very end of it, was where everything happened. Out on the wide expanse of water it might sometimes appear that very little was going on but the pond was a place of secrets. It was dotted with reed-covered islands. Around the edges there were many other hidden places, quiet pools and secluded channels. And it was here that many of the shyer birds lived in perfect seclusion.

I doubt if they would ever have admitted it but one of the delights of the pond for the swallows was the knowledge that as they flew high in the sky above it admiring eyes were watching them secretly from below. It was now late summer and all the young swallows were strong and experienced flyers. Early in the morning and again at dusk they would dart about the sky above the pond feeding on flying insects. Often, if they were feeding under the shade of the trees which grew around the edge of it, all that could be seen of them were their creamy breasts, pale threads of light in the gloom. And although they never ever collided with each other, that is not to say that accidents never happened.

You see, one of their most spectacular stunts involved taking a drink of water while still in flight and that was how Wake had first met the duck. Skimming in low, on a morning when the surface was unusually choppy, he had failed to notice two pink legs and a tuft of tail just above the water. With his beak open in the act of taking a sip of water from the pond he struck the only visible portion of a duck.

It would probably have been all right if the duck had not attempted to gulp in surprise while his beak was still under the water; a beak, let me say, designed by nature to scoop up prodigious quantities of whatever happens to be going, in this case water. Bubbles burst to the surface, hinting at some awful crisis down below and then the duck's indignant features followed them up.

"I do beg your pardon," he warbled, in a watery sort of way, as a substantial quantity of the contents of the pond cascaded down his face, in a highly complicated fountain. "Was I ignoring you? I'm afraid I was miles away... under the water actually. Ducks do it all the time but I'm sure it could be stopped if you insist."

Now though, that little incident had been put behind them and they were friends, or at least as friendly as a swallow and a duck can ever really hope to be.

It was the afternoon when Wake alighted on a strand of wire on a decaying boundary fence running right down into the pond. Alongside him, too full to move, two young swallows lolled sleepily in the warm sunlight, waiting impatiently for the pangs of hunger to return, so that they could continue with their most agreeable instructions. Soon afterwards the duck came floating serenely across the water and greeted him.

"You'll be getting off soon then," said the duck. "Won't be long now?"

"A couple of weeks actually." Wake tried to look sympathetic. "Sorry you can't come in a way."

The duck shook his head and steadied himself under the water with his webbed feet, as the movement threatened to leave him looking backwards.

"Don't you worry about us. We'll manage. We'd sooner stop here actually, even though it will probably freeze over and we'll be stuck down at one end, like last winter."

Wake found it hard to accept that the duck was not envious. The swallows would soon be leaving. They would not have to endure the cold and the dark which the older birds kept warning them were coming closer every day, with the approach of the mysterious time called winter. They would be flying away to live under the sun, until the weather improved. The ducks, on the other hand, like many other birds living around the pond, were obliged to stay.

"Is it the flying?" Wake inquired solicitously. "Is that why you don't go? You're not awfully good at flying, I notice."

Wake was being tactful. In his view the ducks were quite terrible at flying. They seemed to fly only in emergencies and when they did so it was invariably in a straight line, with a strained expression on their faces. Landing always seemed to come as an enormous relief to them and when at length they did crash down the whole pond resounded, with the result that some of the more nervous birds scattered into the air and refused to return until they had received firm assurances about the ducks' future conduct.

"Actually, I have got this thing about flying," the duck agreed, "and flying where you're going would really terrify me. If I have to fly somewhere else I like to be able to see it from where I am; preferably clearly. You certainly can't see the place you're going to from here."

Wake had often tried to imagine the place they were going to, somewhere so far away that only the swallows had ever been there. There was only one place he knew like that. He had glimpsed it from time to time throughout the summer when flying very high. It was the place where the sky came right down to meet the land. That was obviously as far as anyone could go; and it must be there that the swallows spent the winter.

All this time the two baby swallows had been lolling in the sun alongside him. Each of them had consumed about three breakfasts and now they were both fast asleep, smiling in a way which suggested they were dreaming of lunch. When one of them rolled off the strand of wire and plopped plumply into the water the duck did not seem greatly surprised, as though he had seen it all before. Gliding rapidly across the surface of the pond, he took the protesting infant in his strong yellow beak and quickly put him back, alongside his companion who had slept on undisturbed throughout this little emergency.

"This business of fattening up the youngsters. Very odd. Isn't there any food where you're going?"

This much Wake did know about the Crossing. "It isn't for when we get there," he explained. "It's for the journey. Apparently there isn't any food when we're crossing the sea."

All the time they had been talking the sun had been bright in the sky and sparkling on the water, but at that moment it went behind a cloud. The surface of the pond darkened and in the sudden gentle breeze the reeds began to bend and rustle and Wake found that he was shivering.

"I have a feeling," said the duck," that you will be leaving very soon and since you will be travelling over the sea why don't you have a word with the gulls?"

Wake had never actually been to the estuary before and his first thought on arriving there was that some birds really did live lives which were very odd indeed when you compared them with swallows. Instead of a barn and a forest, with a pond at the edge of it, the gulls inhabited a place where it was clear there was nothing to see and nothing to do.

The estuary was flat and wide and its sands stretched away to the distant shore, shimmering and silent in the drowsy afternoon sunshine. Here and there he could see the watery gleam of numerous wide pools, so shallow and still that the ribbed sands could clearly be seen beneath the surface. Around several of the pools little groups of gulls were quietly gossiping, in a bored sort of way. On the far side of the estuary, just below the line of green where the land began again, he could just detect a silvery thread of water. This, he assumed, must be the sea.

Feeling distinctly nervous about addressing such a large gathering, Wake singled out a gull who was lounging at the edge of one of the pools, a little apart from the others, staring vacantly into space.

"Pardon me," he said diffidently, "but would that be the sea over there?"

There was a mortifying splutter of amusement from a group of younger gulls standing a little distance away but the one he had addressed did not laugh.

"Not exactly," said the gull, in a grave but friendly manner. "It's more what we round here call a river."

Wake felt even more embarrassed. He knew perfectly well what a river looked like. It was simply that he had been expecting to see the sea. Aware that the younger gulls had fallen silent and were listening intently, to be sure of enjoying his next indiscretion, he tried to explain.

"I'll be leaving with the other swallows very soon and as you know we have to cross the sea. Since I've never actually seen it I was just wondering what it looked like. I thought it would be here in the estuary."

"The sea?" The gull seemed to ponder the idea. "Well, it has been here once today and it will be coming again, but we never really know exactly when. To be perfectly honest it seems to please itself." He turned to his companions. "Anyone know when the sea's due back?"

Wake had never in his life before beheld an argument like the one which now broke out among the little group of gulls. It was clear that the peaceful scene had been highly deceptive; the gulls had merely been passing the time while they awaited the opportunity to quarrel about something and he had provided it. Basically the argument seemed to centre upon exactly when the sea had last been in the estuary and therefore when it could be expected to return. What he found quite appalling was the spectacle of so much ill-feeling being generated over such a simple matter.

Some of the gulls sprang into the air screaming. Others opened their wings and rushed at each other along the sands. One of them was so provoked by the controversy that he snatched a small fish from the beak of the bird he was quarrelling with and fled away with the victim in hot pursuit. Wake had never seen so much anger before over so little but the extra-ordinary thing about it was how quickly the gulls recovered their composure. Within seconds they were all softly conversing together again, as though nothing had happened, and there was no indication that anyone was sulking.

"I'm afraid no one seems very sure," said the gull apologetically, "but if you hang around you're sure to see it. It comes in most days, although it always seems to be at a different time."

Wake felt that perhaps explanations were in order, if only because he considered himself indirectly responsible for the scene he had just witnessed. The gull listened intently as he described the excitement among the younger swallows, their eagerness to take part for the first time in the great adventure of the Crossing. The gull seemed so interested that he even talked about the sea.

"I've never actually seen it and I wondered if it was anything like the pond."

"The sea is not like the pond," said the gull grimly. "The sea is not like anything. There is only one sea and it is enough."

He pointed away down the shimmering flat surface of the sands, stretching away empty and still into the far distance where the blue haze of the sky curved down to the ground.

"Don't let this fool you. In a few hours time you won't know this place. The sea is just waiting out there. It is always waiting. It'll be waiting for you swallows when you go." A thought seemed to occur to him and he studied Wake with rather embarrassing intensity. "You swallows are very small, aren't you... much smaller than I thought? I just hope you all make it across."

Wake flew back towards the barn through an evening light he had never seen before. Dark clouds were rolling in across the sky directly above him but down on the western horizon the sun was still a brilliant glare. There was a strange rumbling sound all around the sky and as he sped home just above the ground the wind began to rise and stir the yellow fields of grain below, so that they seemed to shake with little shivers of foreboding. For the first time in his life, as he flew home alone in the long evening light, Wake became sad with the knowledge of change.

On impulse he decided to call in at the rookery on his way back to the barn, knowing that the rooks would cheer him up, as they always did. As usual he could hear them long before he saw them. It was widely accepted that of all the birds living around the estuary the rooks were the least musical. When other birds were trying to think of something complimentary to say about their singing they were usually reduced to discussing their phrasing, that is to say the intervals which occurred between the actual notes; if asked by the rooks for an honest opinion of their musical talents they would lavishly praise the charm of these silences and urge that they be lengthened. Once a group of rooks had actually been persuaded to squawk just once and remain silent for half an hour before concluding the performance with a brief croak. Everyone agreed that this had been a musical breakthrough and worthy of every encouragement.

These artistic doubts, however, were not shared by the rooks. They were aware that no other bird anywhere in the forest sounded quite like them but they had come to believe that this was because their musical talents were so remarkable. (This is a common mistake, made by many artistes who find they are without imitators.)

Sometimes, when the weather was particularly pleasant, the blackbirds would announce one of their popular summer evening recitals. These were always much enjoyed by the other birds who would all fall silent to listen as those perfect notes rang like tiny bells through the warm stillness of the forest night. Whenever this happened the rooks would listen with respectful sympathy, secure in the knowledge that the sound was nothing like the one which they produced. For this and other reasons many of the more elegant birds in the forest refused to have anything to do with the rooks. Even Wake's mother had been heard to say that they "lowered the tone". And it was precisely because everyone tended to look down on them that the rooks built their nests higher than anyone else.

"At least," they would say, when they had suffered some particularly hurtful snub, "when it comes to where people live everyone is beneath *us.*"

But living at the very tops of the tallest trees had one serious disadvantage; it meant that the lives of the rooks were in a permanent state of emergency. The wind was almost always blowing, often reaching gale force, and for much of the time it was raining as well. This meant that the rooks suffered the worst housing conditions in the whole forest. Their strange croaking sound, so unlike the song of any other bird, was directly attributable to the fact that they all suffered from the most awful sore throats, as a result of being almost constantly wet. There are few pleasures in life quite so enjoyable as Getting Out Of Wet Things but the rooks could not do this; they were obliged to sit around in wet feathers for hours on end. They also suffered from another health problem; because their nests were constantly swinging backwards and forwards in the wind their stomachs were in a permanently delicate state.

In the spring there was no more sorry sight in the whole of the forest than a nest filled with newly-hatched rooks, lying there at the very top of a tree, with sore throats and stomach ache, tossed by the wind, soaked by the rain, for hours on end, inexplicably launched into this frantic existence and clinging to the belief that if they could just hang on calm would eventually be restored. In view of their life-style the constant cheerfulness of the rooks was a little strange, to say the least.

With the storm now overhead, it had grown considerably darker and already the first drops of rain were starting to fall. High up in the rookery the wind was hissing through the topmost branches, bending them this way and that, so that the rooks' nests looked like so many frail little boats tossing about on a turbulent sea of green.

And yet the rooks seemed just as cheerful as ever. As Wake arrived one of the younger ones he knew vaguely by sight peered out over the edge of a ramshackle mass of sticks and mud. He looked as tattered and unkempt as the nest in which he lay.

"Hello there," he croaked. "Batten down the hatches, hey? It's going to be a long night." Leaning right over the edge of the nest, he used his beak to manoeuvre one of the sticks into a more secure position. "You'll soon be out of this lot then? I don't blame you. Something tells me it's going to be a long winter."

"I suppose you'd like to be coming with us?" Wake suggested. The rain was now falling quite heavily and the wind was much stronger. In their exposed and rickety nests, lurching and swaying to the accompaniment of loud squawks of despair from the younger birds, the little colony of rooks looked like the survivors of some terrible disaster, cast adrift on wild green seas. "Creakwing says it's never wet where we're going. You would all be nice and dry."

A faint twinge of regret crossed the rook's rainy features. "I sometimes think it would be nice just for once to live somewhere that wasn't moving," he agreed. "Somewhere quite still, where the sun was always shining." He looked at Wake sharply. "Just so long as it was still at the top of the tree, of course." Then his rough croak sank to a throaty whisper and he looked round furtively. "To tell you the truth we're all a bit worried because there does seem to have been a revival of interest in rook pie around these parts recently and from our point of view it doesn't look good. But there are worse things than the wind and the rain, you know; worse even than discovering you're an ingredient in a recipe."

Wake had the feeling that his bedraggled companion was anxious about something. "You do understand, don't you, how long the journey is when you are following the sun? It isn't just over the hill, you know. It takes a long time and sometimes....." His voice trailed away and then all at once he was his old cheery self again. "Still it's probably better than this lot. Sometimes I wonder why rooks weren't born ducks. It would have made a lot more sense."

Later that night as he lay tucked up safe and warm in his nest, Wake listened in awe as the very first storm he had ever experienced raged overhead. All night long the rain came down straight and steady on the roof of the barn. Thunder blundered across in the darkness and in the flashes of lightning he could see

10

his small brothers and sisters peering across at him, as though wondering what he was going to do about it.

They could not see their mother but her voice sought to comfort them. "It won't hurt you. It's only a storm. It's a sign that the summer is nearly over."

Long after the storm had passed away, lying there in his nest at the edge of the forest, he continued to listen to the sound of the rain dripping through the leaves and flowers and from the eaves of the barn, down to the ground below. Tomorrow, Wake told himself, he would go and see Creakwing. With the summer now almost at an end and the Crossing about to begin perhaps the old leader would now explain.

And so he joined his brothers and sisters in sleep. He was still sleeping when a great stillness took the place of the storm. The skies began to clear. The stars appeared and soon afterwards a large moon rose up to hang among them like a dim yellow lamp in the misty night. The swallows still did not stir as the air grew colder and colder. And none of them noticed when for the first time that summer a faint and silvery sheen began to appear on the grass below the barn, gleaming cold and white in the faint light of the moon.

* * *

Chapter 2

Next morning, after some searching and asking around, Wake found Creakwing perched on a telephone wire running across the kitchen garden at the back of the farm. The morning was sunny and warm again after the storm and although the grass under the apple trees was still wet an old armchair had been moved out on to the lawn and the old man who no longer worked was sitting out in it. His eyes were covered by a large silk handkerchief, bright orange in colour with a brilliant yellow sun right in the centre, and he appeared to be fast asleep. Behind him the kitchen window was wide open and inside someone was speaking on the radio.

"Quiet boy," the old leader commanded, even though Wake had not said a word. "I'm trying to find out about the weather."

Wake was astonished. "Here?"

"Where else? Now just keep quiet for a minute. I want to know if it's finally on the turn."

"But I thought...."

"You thought what, boy?"

"I thought that we found out about the weather by sort of studying the signs... the wind and the sky, that sort of thing."

"That's how they used to do it," said Creakwing impatiently. "Now it's a lot easier because we've got weather forecasts. So if you wouldn't mind..."

After listening carefully to the radio for a minute or so Creakwing at last turned his attention to the young swallow, in a manner which could hardly be described as friendly. Wake felt distinctly awkward and uneasy about finding himself alone for the first time with the most famous swallow of all. As he waited for Creakwing to notice him he had been thinking very carefully about what to say first. Several times things occurred to him but he quickly rejected them in favour of something else. Finally he was confident that he had thought of the ideal observation; one which seemed appropriate for the occasion, both informative and respectful and suitable for someone of Creakwing's enormous stature in the community.

"Good Morning," he said. "I'm Wake."

"Are you now?" responded the old leader. "And what is that to me?"

It was not an encouraging beginning. "I just wondered about the storm last night," Wake continued. "Does it really mean that summer is finally over?"

"Does it really mean that summer is finally over?" No one likes having their questions repeated, very slowly and thoughtfully, and Wake was no exception. Clearly he had said something wrong. "Didn't you see the pond this morning? Didn't you notice the leaves on the water? Even a wind like we had last night cannot bring the leaves down until it is time. There is the answer to your question. The summer is indeed finally over."

"What is the winter then?" said Wake boldly. "Won't you please tell me what happens?"

It was there, warm and safe in the quiet kitchen garden, at the end of that unforgettable first summer, that Wake first learned about the changes wrought by winter. For some reason he did not at the time understand the legendary leader of the swallows seemed anxious to talk. His initial hostility disappeared and yet as he spoke it began to seem as though he was no longer aware that anyone was listening. Beneath his words there was also something else; the strongest and the bravest of the swallows seemed sad.

The only sound was a soft rustling high above them as the wind played in the leaves at the tops of the trees. Below them in the garden the thickly clustered flowers drowsed in a waxy stillness. The only movement seemed to come from the bright orange handkerchief on the old man's face, as it billowed softly up and down in time with his breathing.

Could it really be true that this peaceful scene was about to change? And yet that was what the old leader was saying. The wind was going to change; the sky, too; even the sun would be different. Soon the ground would be heaped with something white called snow; it sounded like apple blossom, only for some reason it was cold. The leaves would fall in the forest so that there was no shade and no shelter. The pond would become cold and hard so that no birds could drink from it. There would be no food for birds like them. And if they stayed they would die.

"What happens if you die?" Wake inquired politely, but the old leader did not seem to hear.

There were really only two kinds of birds, he said; those who stayed and those who went away. No one knew how it happened that some birds had two homes and the others only one. The swallows, though, had two homes and that was where they were going --to their other home.

Creakwing described the journey they would undertake and as he did so Wake was not aware that he was speaking of things not usually mentioned in the presence of very young swallows. Even if everything went well it would be a long journey, across seas and mountains and not all the swallows who left would find their way to their winter home. There would be dangers from humans and from other birds, fierce and pitiless, which it seemed would be waiting for them far to the south. When Creakwing spoke of humans Wake found himself remembering the legend of the Crossing during which the old leader had suffered at their hands. the memorable day when he and a little group of swallows had saved the Crossing from disaster by deliberately flying low to attract the attention of men firing at them with guns from the ground below. The main body of swallows had flown on unscathed but all who took part in that heroic exploit had been lost, apart from Creakwing .[3]

The more he listened to the old leader describing the journey the more convinced Wake became that it would be enormously easy to get lost.

"Will someone show us the way?" he inquired.

They would not fly alone, Creakwing explained. Very soon the swallows who had all lived apart during the long months of summer would assemble for the first and only time in one vast roost and soon afterwards they would all leave together. It would not be necessary for Wake to know the way; all he was required to do was follow. Creakwing seemed to sense his concern.

"You'll be all right. You'll all be all right. You can tell your mother: 'Any day now'."

With these words he was gone but Wake did not follow. He remained alone on the telephone wire thinking about the old leader's words. Something was puzzling him; two things actually. Firstly, wasn't there something rather odd about the way Creakwing

---

[3] *As you will appreciate Creakwing earned his own fame name as a result of that exploit but a bureaucratic mix-up so delayed his naming ceremony that by the time he came to be honoured, the nickname Creakwing had become too popular to be abandoned. Just for the record his fame name was Horatio. Your parent, or guardian, or even a knowledgeable teacher, will tell you why this was especially appropriate.*

had said: "You'll be all right. You'll all be all right?" Why not: "*We'll* be all right?" Secondly, as he had watched Creakwing fly away, it had seemed to him that there was something unusual about his movements; usually a swallow flew like a wave, swooping and soaring, but that morning he had seen something different. The old leader had flown awkwardly. Once or twice his wings had fluttered and he had faltered in the sky; something was wrong.

The longest telephone wire in the neighbourhood was the one running all the way from the lane to the farm. Often you would see several swallows perched on it taking the air but that evening was different. When Wake arrived almost every inch of the wire was occupied. Scores and scores of swallows were roosting there; darting up into the air and down again; constantly changing position; at the same time the air was filled with a loud and excited twittering. The best way to describe the noise is to say that it was remarkably similar to the sort of cries of joy and wonder you hear whenever two prams meet. You see, for the first time that summer all the mothers of all the swallows were finally together, all in one place. And that was the reason for the excitement. Since none of them had seen each other's offspring until that moment it was necessary to indulge in a great deal of boasting about infant swallows which to an unbiased observer seemed remarkably similar in appearance. Wake was quickly caught up in the rejoicing.

"This is Wake," cried his mother, as soon as he arrived alongside her on the wire. He could not help feeling most uncomfortable as the other mothers dutifully studied him with expressions on their faces which most of you will be familiar with. It is very hard to know where to look while being admired in this merciless way and Wake was no exception.

But since that evening all the young birds up and down the wire were being fondly displayed by their mothers, this might be a good time to meet the other swallows who will become important as the story of the famous Crossing unfolds. Wake you know; the others (in no particular order of importance) were Oliver and his sister Winnie; Harold and his sister, Bess, and Bony. [4]

---

[4] *I am sure that the more knowledgeable among you will quickly identify the celebrated historical figures who provided the inspiration for these fame names. I should just point out, though, that in the case of Winnie a mistake had occurred. For some reason it was assumed that this was a*

All along the wire, on that lovely evening as summer finally came to an end, the mother birds were chattering wildly. Most of it was boasting about offspring and nests and the view from the window and how absolutely wonderful everything was in every conceivable way. Here and there some fathers had also turned up on the off-chance that there might just be some compliments going spare. The mothers were particularly pleased to see them, as it afforded a wonderful opportunity to ignore them completely, since they had spent the greater part of the summer having fun high in the sky and being far from supportive. In fact some of the fathers were being introduced to their offspring for the very first time, an honour which did not appear to have induced the sort of rapture being experienced by the mothers; some of the fathers, looked distinctly disappointed, even a bit wary.

Some very young birds were adding to the general excitement by performing a trick they had learned only that summer. They would fall forward from the wire with their feet gripping it tightly, so that they whizzed round in a complete circle to arrive back precisely where they had started.

Creakwing was perched in the middle of the sagging wire, with a short distance between him and the swallows perched on either side, as a mark of respect, seemingly untroubled by the tremendous noise going on all around him and exhibiting a tolerance of manner reminiscent of the more decent sort of headmaster at assembly on the first day back at school after the holidays. Until all at once it changed.

"Now hear this," he bawled without warning. "Just settle down."

High in the bright blue air three swallows, twittering excitedly as they practiced near misses suddenly remembered why they were there and zoomed in to settle on the telephone wire which now sagged under the weight of all those birds and then at last there was stillness and silence.

Creakwing spoke briskly. "You all know why we are here. The Crossing begins tomorrow night." All along the wire there was an excited twittering which he quelled with an upraised wing. "I just want to mention a few points. Older birds will excuse me if this is familiar stuff but it is important.

girl's name whereas the opposite was most definitely the case.

"First of all--your leaders. You all know who your leaders are, so follow them. Wherever they lead you, follow them, night and day, until the journey is over. They have been carefully chosen. There are things they know which the rest of you do not. Respect them and follow them.

"Now a word about flying. From now on, until the Crossing is over, all fancy flying is cancelled. For the next few days you can forget about near-misses.. free-falling and single combat." Creakwing gazed in each direction along the wire, as though aware that his next words would create something of a sensation. "From now until the Crossing is over you will fly in a straight line. Like the ducks." This, of course, was just too much for some of the younger swallows. All along the wire they turned sideways and stared at each other very hard with great seriousness to see who could be made to laugh first. One or two spluttered. Creakwing's eyes silenced them. "I repeat: you fly like ducks, in a straight line, in the new way you have been taught." And then he added mildly: "If you fool about and you find your companions have all gone over the next hill there is a very good chance that you will never be heard of again."

It really was extraordinary to perceive how the swallows who had been so attentive from the moment he began to speak seemed to be growing even more still and silent as they continued to listen.

"If you notice a bird which is in difficulty.. if you see someone straggling, tell your leader and then fly on. Do not stop or even pause. He or she will do whatever is necessary. You must stay with the group. When it is time to pass over the sea keep even closer together and try not to look down. The sea is not for swallows." Creakwing seemed to sense that his last words had troubled some of the younger birds, so much so that their parents were smiling at them re-assuringly.

"I am delighted to see that many of you are now disgustingly fat." At this observation the mood became distinctly merrier. "I can assure you that when the Crossing is over you will all be very thin indeed." Smiles of relief from the more weight-conscious female birds. He paused again and his gaze gently mocked their solemn concentration. "Don't look so alarmed. You will be all right. Just remember to make sure you don't leave with the wrong group. There was a young swallow long ago who managed to get attached to the warblers and flew to the sun with them. He had to stay with them all winter and when he came back he thought he was a warbler. It took days of careful counselling from a very pretty swallow to change his mind." Creakwing raised his voice above the delighted laughter. "So be careful who you fly with. And remember --you leave tomorrow. By the light of the stars."

Ever afterwards Wake was to remember that the old leader's voice did not change or falter at this moment. He merely paused imperceptibly before making his announcement; the momentous announcement which would change Wake's life and create from his exploits and those of his companions a story which would be told and loved in the telling as long as there were dark nights and warm nests and swallows to listen.

"I shall not be leading on this occasion," said Creakwing casually. "My wing has been giving me a few problems and I don't want to slow the Crossing down, so I'll follow on at my own speed in a few days' time."

* * *

Chapter 3

I do think I ought to point out for the benefit of the more nervous among you that in fact there was very little danger of a swallow joining the warblers' migration by mistake. The whole thing was far too well-organised for that to happen. And once more, as in the case of weather forecasts on the wireless, the explanation lies in the fact that the swallows had lived among men (or rather above them) for a very long time and had learned to use the knowledge they had gained.

One of the things they had observed while man-watching was the ability of humans to organise movements on a grand scale, for the curious purpose of fighting one another. On their long journeys to and from their winter and summer homes the migrant birds had flown over vast armies on countless occasions. They had observed that the secret of moving large groups across enormous distances was planning. Over the years the groups controlled by men had become larger and larger and the distances they traversed greater and greater. While deploring the causes which brought these vast gatherings together and hoping that one day they would happen for purely social reasons the birds had been deeply impressed by the organisation required and had learned to copy it.

For many years now Creakwing had been involved in that planning and so the morning after the roost of the swallows he set off for his final briefing before the Crossing began. Since all the migrant birds left at roughly the same time the occasion was important because it ensured that everything went smoothly.

The briefings were always held at the same secret location just inside the forest and all the migrant birds attended, with one exception. The cuckoos were not welcome; there was something about them. Dark suspicion surrounded the cuckoos and although nothing had ever been satisfactorily proved they were not trusted and always kept very much to themselves. I will not tell you what they were suspected of (that is a task for your mother, or some other close relative) but it was not pleasant.

That morning, though, Creakwing saw that all the other familiar migrant birds were represented; there were swifts, warblers, redstarts, chiff chaffs, flycatchers, martins and many more, all of them quiet and thoughtful, as they perched along the wire of a sagging fence around the overgrown wastes of what had once been a kitchen garden.

Creakwing was even more thoughtful than the others. For the first time in all the years since he had become a Grand Leader he now found himself thinking rather more about himself than about the swallows he was responsible for. Lately his wing had been giving him a great deal of trouble; foraging for food had become a considerable effort. It wasn't simply his age; it was the wound he had suffered on that day long ago when men had opened fire with guns on the column of swallows taking part in the Winter Crossing. As the legend eternally reminded them, he and a little group of volunteers had flown to the rear of the flock and swooped low over the guns, to distract the men who were trying to kill them. This remarkable action was successful. The men turned all their fire on the gallant little band while the rest of the flock flew on unharmed. To his great surprise, in view of the fate of all of his companions, he was hit only once, as the shot from the guns swept up through the towering silence of that sunny afternoon long ago.

The wound he sustained that day had healed a long time ago but over the years the wing had become increasingly stiff and painful. He was still able to forage for food in the immediate vicinity; occasionally he could travel longer distances on those days when the cold and the rain made food harder to find. But towards the end of the Spring Crossing that year there had been moments when he had doubted his ability to complete the journey and now it was about to start all over again. Africa had never seemed so far away and yet he knew that every day the time they called winter was coming closer. Winter was quite beyond their experience; a transformation so terrible that the swallows had retreated from it long ago. Sometimes at the end of summer, just as they prepared to leave, the swallows would sense winter's dark shadow approaching from the east and then they would shudder to think that they had almost left it too late.

The swallows could not understand why all the birds did not flee each year to warmer and kinder skies, leaving tyrannical winter to rant and rage in angry disappointment through the bare and empty countryside. Those species which did stay seldom spoke of their experiences to the migrant birds when they came back in the spring but it was not necessary, for it was always plain to see that many of the birds they had left behind were not there when they returned.

All these thoughts passed through the old swallow's mind as Supreme Leader went through the final details of the Crossing. This year the honour had been bestowed on a lady willow warbler. It was very much a ceremonial role; the willow warbler was, of course, a leader like Creakwing and all she was required to do was to preside over their final meeting. In effect this involved summarising the plans they had already agreed and then SAYING A FEW WELL-CHOSEN WORDS.

The willow warbler reminded them that the scout birds had already left. (It was their task to locate any favourable feeding grounds along the way and identify any unforeseen dangers lying in their path.) She summarised all the available information about wind direction and strength, cruising speeds and altitudes and the final timings for all the departures due to take place over the next few days. Creakwing heard her mention that this year his group would be among the very first to leave but he was not really listening. He had rehearsed the plans with his own leaders so many times that they were now totally familiar.

But there was one final custom to be observed. Before he left Creakwing drew the Supreme Leader to one side and told her, and only her, what he planned to do. She replied in the time-honoured and traditional way: "I wish you a good winter and trust to see you in the spring." But her eyes were informal and sad.

The forest was now in the grip of an extraordinary excitement; the excitement of the imminent miracle of migration. Even the swallow leaders who had seen it all before were affected. Overhead in the sky and all along the wires the swallows were massing. It was as though their individual wills had ceased to exist; whether roosting or circling in great clouds overhead they had merged into one great and irresistible intention.

In all the excitement the news that Creakwing would not be leaving with the main group was not seen as greatly unusual. So far as any of them knew he meant what he said; he would simply be leaving a few days after the main migration, once his wing was feeling better. If any of the older, wiser birds suspected anything they did not mention it; birds are a great deal more discreet than they are given credit for.

On that last evening summer was an old but lovely lady about to leave and softly close the door behind her. All day the sun shone down on the swallows' final preparations and as night fell it stood like a bowl of bubbling gold on the flat horizon. Long after it had gone the pink light still lay in painted streaks across the purple sky. The swallows waited. They waited as the gulls returned home across an estuary as flat as glass, flying so low that the surface of the wide, still water mirrored their shape and seemed to suggest that other ghostly birds were also going home beneath the water. They waited as the rooks settled down to sleep, grateful to find the world so calm again. The light grew fainter. Now it seemed that only the swallows were still awake. All along the curve of the wire, motionless, they waited.

And then a mist began to rise from the ground and billow softly across the field at the edge of the forest. Higher and higher it rose towards them and then finally, as though the rolling mist was floating them away, the swallows rose silently through the dim light and in a moment they had gone, disappearing into the darkness of the southern sky and taking summer with them.

Creakwing slept uneasily that night and early next morning he flew to the pond to feed. Even though his mind was filled with the knowledge that the swallows had gone there was perhaps just a chance that one or two of them had delayed their departure, for reasons he could not begin to imagine. If that was so he could perhaps rebuke them and then have a little chat before sending them on their way. But he was the only swallow there.

After breakfast he perched on the old wire fence leading down into the water. It would not have pleased him to know that he looked sad but he did. He found himself remembering the summer and wondering if perhaps he had sometimes been a little hard on the very young ones. They would be well on their way by now, getting nearer to the sun every hour. He was not exactly lonely because the pond was busy with resident birds, but it felt as though he was the last swallow in the world and this feeling served only to remind him that from now on every day would bring some new change, some alteration quite beyond his experience. For him the winter lay ahead like an unknown land.

To judge the effect of what happened next you have to understand that for all its charms a pond is a pretty uneventful sort of place. Nothing very memorable happens there and this means that after feeding a lot of birds tend to hang around all day, with time on their hands, hoping there will be some sort of INCIDENT, something to talk about. Anything which is just a little out of the ordinary tends to be discussed for days and what happened next certainly served to dispel a little of the tedium from some pretty humdrum lives.

High in the sky above the pond, long after it was widely understood that they had all left for the southern sun, six swallows appeared and flew straight down to alight on the old wire fence alongside Creakwing. Startled as he was, the old leader realised that he actually knew one of them. "We couldn't let you stay here all alone." Wake's eyes were ablaze with excitement. He gazed proudly along the wire at his little band who nodded harmoniously. "So we decided to stay here with you until you're ready to make the Crossing and then we can all leave together."

* * *

23

Chapter 4

I am well aware that in later years when the birds living around the estuary first started to learn about the Winter Crossing all the accounts of it tended to be very solemn and dignified in their efforts to describe the moment when Wake came to his momentous decision to remain behind, after the main migration had left. I have even heard it suggested that at one stage he went alone to a solitary vantage point where he spent many hours in quiet reflection, before returning to the barn and gathering his faithful five around him. Quite untrue. At that stage in his life Wake never thought very much about anything. The evidence for this is there in the fact that the question most frequently addressed to him in those days was "What on earth did you do that for?" The truth of the matter is that he genuinely believed that they would be delayed for only a few days until Creakwing's strength had returned and what he actually suggested to his companions was that it would be fun to escape briefly from the supervision of their parents by keeping him company.

It was easy, really. All they did was to make sure that every time their mothers looked for them on the evening of departure they were very prominently visible doing something ridiculous. Re-assured by this bad behaviour, their mothers simply assumed in the bustle and excitement of departure that all six of them were flying together. After all, they were now several months old and supposed to act their age, as the saying goes.

As the main group turned on course for the south the six simply peeled off in the gloom of the summer night and disappeared into the woods. Wake took the added precaution of ensuring that they remained concealed all night, so that when they revealed themselves to Creakwing the main party would be so far away that he could not possibly order them to leave. The old leader listened in silence to the details of their noble gesture and then he gave judgement.

"Without exception you are all fools," he pronounced. The fools inspected one another. "Six of the most foolish swallows in the history of the species." Five of the fools inspected the sixth who had thought of the idea. "You say that you stayed behind to keep me company. What would you say if I told you that you might very well find that you have to stay here for ever?"

It was there for the very first time, on that familiar perch beside the pond, where they had spent so many thoughtless hours all through that glorious summer, that a little seriousness at last entered the lives of the six young swallows. They listened in silence as Creakwing revealed what none of the others had been told; he had no intention of making the Winter Crossing; he would be staying.

High above them the morning sky was empty. Many other migrant birds had also departed during the night and they had never known the pond to be so silent. It seemed as though they were the only swallows remaining anywhere in the land. From time to time they attempted to interrupt but Creakwing silenced them with a weary impatience they had never seen before.

He told them about the pain and stiffness of his crippled wing and his belief that his strength could no longer sustain him on such an arduous journey. He insisted that he would be all right; lots of resident birds stayed beside the pond all through the winter and most of them were still there when the swallows returned in the spring. Because they had so foolishly failed to depart with the main migration, he said, they would have to leave alone, but he would not allow them to leave without instruction; no harm would come to them.

Gradually over the next few days Wake, too, became much more serious about things. And was quietly grateful for the fact that Creakwing never once reminded him how foolish he had been. He was also secretly pleased to notice how Creakwing seemed to assume that he was in charge of their little group. Most mornings he would order the others to go off foraging for food. "You are going to have to build your strength up even more, now that you've been left behind," he would say. But on some mornings he would order Wake to remain behind, saying: "We have things to talk about."

On these occasions the two would sit talking for hours on the fence running down to the pond. Wake began to look forward to these private moments; he loved having the legendary Creakwing all to himself and was secretly glad that the others were not there to share in their discussions about the problems of leadership. And all the time it seemed that the older bird was testing him in some mysterious way.

"It isn't enough just to want to be at the front," Creakwing observed one afternoon. "There is a lot more to being a leader than that. Humans can choose just about anyone to lead them because so far as I can see they usually aren't going anywhere, but it's different for swallows. We get lots of applications, as you can imagine, and since no one would want to be a leader if they had the intelligence to know how hard it really is we choose only from among those who do not apply. It does rather simplify matters."

Creakwing also explained how being a leader of swallows meant worrying about others but not too much. "Many of the swallows who have just left will never see Africa. It is something that must be accepted. It is the way things are."

He spoke of the dangers the little party would have to face... the perils of the sea... the storms and strong winds which could scatter them all over the sky.. the men who knew their airy paths and lay in wait for them with guns... the fierce birds which hungered for their flesh... and almost at the end of their journey the soft warm nest of the desert waiting to enfold them for ever.

Wake listened intently. He was not exactly frightened. It would be more accurate to say he was worried about the possibility of making a mistake and he wondered if that was how a leader was expected to feel. How wonderful it must be, he thought, to lead a group of swallows through all those dangers and bring them safely home to Africa, possibly to loud applause.

Every day Creakwing talked to him about some new aspect of the journey. He seemed determined to overlook no single detail before sending the young and leaderless swallows on their long journey. They spent one whole day on the single subject of the weather; the way it could change in an instant; what to do in high winds, dense fog or extreme cold; and when to stop flying altogether and wait for things to improve.

One omission puzzled him increasingly, as the hours passed in Creakwing's company without it ever being mentioned. He could not understand why these long, repetitive and sometimes tedious lessons never seemed to touch upon the most important topic of all, the piece of information which was absolutely vital if he was to successfully lead the swallows on that long and hazardous journey to the sun. And so one morning when he was once more alone with Creakwing he decided to mention it.

"When," he asked, "will you tell me how we find the way to Africa?"

There was a brief silence and then the older swallow gave a weary smile which strongly conveyed the impression that he had heard the question many times before.

"I will not be telling you the way. When the time comes if you are truly a leader you will *know* the way; if you are not then I am very much afraid you will not find Africa."

Day after day the explanations and the instructions went on. Sometimes Creakwing showed impatience when he failed to understand something he had said; at other times he became positively angry.

"I just wish you would listen," he exploded one morning. "It is your fault, not mine, that you are still here. I should be out making my own plans for the winter, not worrying about you."

Wake did not reply, for Creakwing's outburst had re-inforced a growing anxiety. It was the first thing he had ever had to worry about. And when you realise why he was so troubled in those final days of autumn you will understand in whose mind the incredible idea of the Winter Crossing first took shape. Wake was beginning to realise that he at least could never leave the old leader behind, to face the coming perils all alone. It was a conviction which became stronger with each passing day, as everything which was dear and familiar to the swallows began to change. These changes are familiar enough to you but try to imagine how you would feel if you lived in a land where winter was coming for the very first time. No swallow in living memory and possibly a great deal longer than that had ever seen the things the swallows were now witnessing.

First there were the trees. All through the warm days of summer their brightly coloured leaves and blossom had blown in the wind like joyful banners, proclaiming their grace and beauty, but now new shapes had replaced the blossom, shapes which lurked among the leaves, dark and still, so that the branches leaned down under the weight of them. Some of these mysterious objects had fallen to the grass below and Wake was interested to see blackbirds, tits and other birds pecking away at them with every sign of pleasure. There was, he thought, no accounting for taste.

One particular tree seemed to symbolise the slow decay occurring all around them; the great beech tree grew at the end of the lane leading up to the farm. All through the summer it had stood there, breasting into the wind with billowing leaves, dipping and rising like a great, green ship, but now it lay becalmed in the still, cold air and here and there dark birds hunched like spiders in its bare branches.

In the mornings now the swallows would often wake up stiff and cold. Sometimes in the night a mist would come down so that when they awoke their view from the barn was obscured; for a few hours everywhere would lie drenched in dew until the sun broke through to betray a conspiracy of glistening spiders' webs hidden among the bushes of the farm garden. Even when the mist had gone the sun shone faintly and the air was chill.

To Wake it was now almost impossible to remember what a wonderfully busy and happy place the pond had once been. Had there really been a bright warm morning in summer when he had collided with a submerged duck while practising how to drink on the wing? How the old place had changed; he specially missed the swifts, so often their aerial companions and even more skilful fliers than the swallows. The swifts dwelt in the air; they lived and ,it was said, even died on the wing. Only the swallows were ever able to come close enough to converse with them but now they were gone; they had been among the first migrants to leave, circling higher and higher in the sky and finally vanishing from sight, absorbed again into the air from which they came.

All the time new birds were arriving from the north to take their place on the pond. Wake had never seen birds like them. Their eyes were bleak and cold and their manner unfriendly. It was as though the icy lands from which they came had frozen everything inside them.

"Don't mind them," said his friend, the duck. "They even scare us a little bit and we see them every year."

Creakwing seemed strangely disturbed by the new arrivals. "I've seen a lot of things in the last few weeks, odd things I never expected to see and what's more I never thought I'd see them in the company of a lot of young swallows," he said one morning. And gazing at Wake in a thoughtful sort of way, he added: "You know, I think you've been delaying, boy. I don't know why and I don't care but I'm telling you now that you must be away by the end of this week--at the very latest. Otherwise you may never leave."

It was true. Wake had been making excuses to delay their departure because his anxiety about the old leader was growing stronger every day. With so many startling changes taking place all around him he was at last learning why the swallows fled from this grim land every winter. How could they leave Creakwing behind to face these dangers alone? It was clear that one of his biggest problems was going to be food; after all, this was mainly why the swallows flew south every winter and he and his companions were already discovering that food was increasingly hard to find. Every day, in attempting to obey Creakwing's instructions to eat as much as they could, they were having to fly ever farther away from the barn.

Not that Creakwing gave any indication that he was worried about his own chances of surviving winter. Alone in his predicament, their leader persisted in making jokes about the coming ordeal, insisting that he was looking forward to having a bit of time to himself. But Wake was not deceived. There were many things he did not know about winter but one thing he did know was that it was no laughing matter.

It was now clearly time to seek some advice about Creakwing's chances; the problem was trying to decide who to ask. All the other migrants had gone and there were very few friendly birds still remaining around the pond. There was really only the duck and although he valued the duck as a companion he hesitated to raise such important matters with one who was so frivolous in appearance. What he needed was a more serious bird, preferably one with a worried frown and a grave manner; a bird which seldom smiled and never ever laughed; one which was renowned for long silences; a bird with that indefinable air of anxiety displayed by those who know far more than they will ever understand. Wake knew of only one bird which fitted that description.......

* * *

Chapter 5

Wake who had never met the tawny owl before found him sitting outside his home in a tree at the edge of the forest. Many years before in a great storm an enormous branch had crashed to earth from a large, old oak tree. It had happened so long ago that the branch was now almost hidden in the tangle of undergrowth below, but in falling the branch had left a gaping hole in the trunk of the tree and here the owl lived very comfortably indeed, convinced that only an owl would have been clever enough to think of it.

Among the birds who lived around the estuary at that time the tawny owl enjoyed a wide reputation for wisdom, based mainly, it must be said, on his scholarly appearance. Birds with smallish heads looked at the owl's enormous one and just assumed that it must be filled to the brim with unusual and helpful thoughts. The tawny owl also behaved in a way which encouraged confidence. All the other birds spent their days flying about; singing, nesting, feeding, quarrelling. Because this frivolous way of life with its lack of responsibilities sometimes made them feel just a little guilty it was good to know that there was at least one of them who spent the whole day deep in thought, with his eyes closed, gently snoring. As a result, the owl was available throughout the hours of daylight for consultations, usually by appointment.

Wake alighted at the edge of the hole where the owl was sitting with his eyes closed and was just about to introduce himself when the owl addressed *him*.

"Next."

Wake looked around just to be sure but there was no one else there. "I'm sorry if I woke you," he said. "Perhaps I could come back."

"I do hope you aren't trying to be sarcastic?" said the owl, with his eyes still tightly closed. Wake was not sure what the word meant but since it had an unpleasant ring to it he denied any such intention.

"Please don't try to take advantage," the owl continued. "For your information owls happen to be able to sleep and think simultaneously. I'll spell it if you like."

Wake was now completely at a loss and so he decided to wait just in case the owl said something he could understand. After a long silence the owl opened his eyes and surveyed him. "You're very quiet today. It's not like you. Are you ill or something?" Wake was even more mystified. "But please sir, I've never been here before."

"What's that got to do with it?" demanded the owl irritably. "Were you as quiet as this yesterday?" Wake had to confess that he couldn't remember. "Of course you weren't, so it isn't like you. Q.E.D. That means Quite Easily Done." The owl looked triumphant. "Now then I wonder if its too much to hope that this time they've sent someone who can provide the right questions for my answers."

"Please sir," said Wake, "I have got some questions but I don't know if they're the right ones."

"Probably not," agreed the owl. "Only time will tell."

Wake was now beginning to wonder if he had come to the right owl. The owl for his part seemed reasonably pleased with the effect he had created. He gazed expectantly at the little swallow and then nodded to indicate that the questions could now commence. Wake moved a little away along the broken branch to make the owl appear a little smaller and started to explain. The owl closed his eyes again and then opened them sharply. "Just concentrating. Carry on."

It is very hard to know where to look when talking to someone who has his eyes closed so Wake addressed his remarks to the trunk above the owl's head. First he explained about Creakwing being unable to fly away on the Crossing because of his injured wing. He reminded the owl that swallows had no knowledge of winter and that already winter was drawing near and he wondered what would happen to the old leader if he was left alone to try to survive the changes which were coming. What, for example, would he eat?

The owl's first question did not appear to have very much to do with any of this.

"Why are *you* still here?" he inquired

Wake launched into another explanation. He told the owl that in fact six swallows had stayed behind altogether but it had all been his idea. (It was strange how what had seemed at first like a proud sort of thing to say now sounded very much like a confession). They had stayed behind to try to help Creakwing on the Crossing but now it seemed that he had never intended to go and was insisting that they must leave without him.

"But I don't think I can leave him behind," he confessed abjectly. "I've tried thinking about it in all kinds of different ways but it always seems wrong."

"And what do the others say?"

"That's why I've come to see you," said Wake. "There is something I need to know, before I talk to the others about what we should do."

"And what were you thinking you might do?."

Wake had actually contemplated listening respectfully to everything the owl said, without interrupting once. He had not planned on doing all the talking himself.

"I was thinking," he said, "that we might stay here with Creakwing until the winter is over."

The owl nodded thoughtfully and said: "And is that your expert opinion?"

"No," said Wake, "that is what I was thinking."

"Thinking, eh? Well, If I were you I'd leave that to the experts," observed the owl loftily. "I automatically assumed that was why you'd come to see me. I assumed you wanted me to do the thinking. All things being equal and in the final analysis."

Humbly, Wake agreed that this was indeed what he had intended. "Now it may surprise you to know that ever since you outlined your problem I have in fact been thinking about it." The owl smiled reassuringly. "You wouldn't have known this because there's nothing much to see but this is the sort of thing I mean. Let us first of all discuss food. The swallows eat insects, I believe, and the problem is that insects disappear in the winter. Correct me if I'm wrong." There was a faintly derisive smile on the owl's features, at this possibility, so Wake merely nodded. "Now let us ask ourselves is it possible that the swallows could learn to change their diet and perhaps eat something else?" His eyes gleamed. "Mice for example."

Wake was about to indicate his willingness to try mouse, perhaps just a little corner, when the owl said: "Please. Don't interrupt. I've only just begun. Let us look at the problem from another viewpoint entirely and consider WHY there are no insects in winter. What happens in winter? All the insects disappear because the weather is so cold. Ideally then we ought to try to ensure that the winter is not so long and a good deal warmer; a tall order admittedly." He looked at Wake sharply. "Do you follow me

32

so far?" Wake said he thought so. "Good. That is another possibility, but there are others. Can we perhaps do something about your food supplies? Can we somehow persuade the insects not to leave for wherever they go, even if it *is* a hard winter? In short is there any inducement we can offer to persuade them to stay?"

"And be eaten?"

"Precisely."

For the first time in his life Wake had come face to face with the awesome power of academic thought on the highest intellectual level and he was beginning to have doubts about his own ability to meet the challenge. Undoubtedly the owl had gone to the heart of the problem and proceeded with scarcely any hesitation to put forward several solutions which were quite remarkable in their ingenuity but implementing them was clearly going to be the hardest part.

"I really am most grateful for your suggestions," he said. "But I wonder if you could just give me some idea how best to carry them out."

"Look," said the owl. "I'm an ideas bird, right? You've just seen that for yourself. How many ideas have I just given you?"

"Three or four?"

"Exactly. Now let's suppose it took me in round figures a quarter of an hour to think of them, although actually I don't think it was that long. Multiply that by four and then multiply that by the number of hours I sit here thinking up ideas every day. And then multiply that by the number of days in a week. Take away the minutes when I'm away hunting mice and how many have you got?" The owl smiled encouragingly as Wake attempted a desperate calculation in his head. "Take your time."

"Forty four?" Wake finally ventured shyly.

"Precisely," confirmed the owl. He looked at Wake with kindly scorn. "So you see that doesn't leave much time for telling people HOW to do things. Anyway those are just a few ideas to be going on with. Do let me know how you get on. Now, you will excuse me, I'm sure. I am rather busy." And with that the owl closed both eyes. A moment later he opened them again. "You could always get one of the bigger birds to carry him there, I suppose. It would make a nice change for one of our resident birds, winter in Africa. Just a thought." Once more silence fell and Wake was just starting to think about leaving when the owl opened his eyes yet again. "Still thinking," he observed sternly but this time when his eyes closed he began to snore gently in a way which did not really suggest intense concentration and as the noise grew steadily louder Wake realised with relief that the owl had run out of inspiration.

On returning to the barn he was pleased to find that his companions were still out foraging for food. He needed to be alone for a time, so that he could give the owl's suggestions the most careful consideration and decide what to do about them. He had just decided to do nothing for the time being when he heard a bird calling his name from outside.

"Do I have the pleasure of addressing the famous leader of the swallows who have stayed behind? And if so is it possible to have a word with him?"

Wake darted to the window and peered out. On a slender branch hanging down from a tree growing close to the barn wall a blue tit was perched. His head was hidden underneath his wing and the whole branch was swinging wildly up and down as he concentrated on preening his feathers. He seemed so unconcerned about anything else that Wake at first wondered if it was the blue tit which had addressed him.

More to attract the blue tit's attention than anything else he said: "I am Wake the swallow who stayed behind. But I'm certainly not famous."

The blue tit at last emerged from under his wing. "Ah, but you are," he assured him. "Your fame has echoed round the forest and if you go on like this they'll be writing songs about you."

Then, apparently realising that his teasing was making Wake uncomfortable, he hopped down on to the sill beside him. "I'm sorry. I know you're worried. But it's true, you know; everyone is talking about the swallows who stayed behind and I just wondered if there was anything I could do to help." He gazed at Wake thoughtfully. "After all, you haven't got much time, have you?"

It really is astonishing how little it takes to make our spirits lift; and admiration will do it every time. If indeed the swallows were becoming famous that was something at least to be going on with, Wake thought to himself. He was also greatly encouraged by the thought that of all the birds in the forest it was a blue tit which had offered to help. He knew all about the tit family. Among the bird population living around the estuary, both resident and migrant, they were widely regarded as the most intelligent and resourceful; in short, a good sort of bird to have around in an emergency.

He began to explain the problem, starting with a few facts relevant to the custom of the swallows of leaving the estuary every winter to escape the cold and gloomy weather.

"It's called migration," interrupted the blue tit impatiently. "I know all about that. Can we just stick to the essentials or we'll still be sitting here talking when spring comes round again?"

Wake resumed his explanation. This time he decided to start with the moment when he first persuaded his five companions to stay behind with him to help Creakwing. The blue tit listened with mounting restlessness, becoming even more impatient when he began to name his companions one by one (it was already becoming clear to Wake how quickly he became bored) and then he interrupted again.

"I don't need names. Everyone knows who you are. It's all over the forest. Just tell me why you went to see the owl this morning?"

Wake stared blankly at this bossy little bird who was beginning to make him feel that up to that very moment he had been merely dawdling his way through life. The blue tit was certainly not what you would call a good listener; in fact listening seemed to irritate him intensely. Wake was now positively wracking his brains to think of something to say which the blue tit did not know already. This time he began by recalling the owl's reputation for wisdom.

"Just tell me what you asked him about and what he said."

It seemed that the only account the blue tit found entirely satisfactory was one which began almost at the very end, because this time he said nothing until, much earlier than planned, Wake finished his story. Then the blue tit hopped from the ledge back on to the branch of the tree and said: "Just give me a minute to think." Wake could not help reflecting that watching the blue tit thinking was not quite so impressive as observing the owl engaged in the same activity, if only because the owl did seem better designed for it, but for some reason he felt a great more confident about the outcome.

"Right," said the blue tit at last. "I want to see you at first light tomorrow. We'll meet in the orchard where we can't be seen from the house. And bring the others with you. There's something I'd like to try out before we go any further." He looked at Wake for confirmation. "OK.?"

Wake was not sure. "Can't you tell me a little more, so that I can tell the others?" The blue tit grinned. "Let us just say that from time to time the owl says something sensible quite by accident and I want to see if by any chance this is one of those occasions. "

* * *

Chapter 6

That night was the coldest the swallows had ever experienced. They slept restlessly and as they slept the first snow fell.

Wake saw it first, on his morning forage in search of food down by the river. Here the landscape widened out and far inland he noticed for the first time the line of hills which curved around to enclose the estuary. The reason he saw them now for the first time was because they were heaped with snow, the first he had ever seen. In the night, like an advancing army creeping forward under the cover of darkness, winter had captured the hills. The distant snow glittered cold and clear and strangely triumphant in the early morning light. You next, it seemed to say.

He arrived in the orchard with his five companions to find the blue tit already there. Creakwing had declined to accompany them.

"You can tell me what he has in mind," he said dismissively. "In any case I'm not used to taking orders from a blue tit, you can tell him from me."

In the chill air of morning the blue tit was being even bossier than usual, for this was his way of keeping warm. "I'm not very pleased," he said ominously. "You would have thought Creakwing, at least, could have been here. After all he is your leader." Wake said nothing and decided not to mention Creakwing's reservations about taking orders from a blue tit. There are some messages which should only be delivered in person and this seemed to be one of them.

"Anyway," began the blue tit briskly, "it seems to me that if Creakwing is going to spend the whole winter here his main problem is going to be food. It's usually possible to keep warm somehow but this whole business of flying away for the winter is basically to do with food. The swallows fly away because their food disappears. Any questions?"

He looked at the swallows impatiently. Since all this was perfectly clear to the swallows and always had been they declined to challenge the blue tit's logic. Privately, Wake was beginning to wonder if he was stuck with the tit equivalent of an owl.

"But the fact remains that lots of other birds do manage to find enough food to survive the winter, including, I may say, the tit family. So what we have to discover is whether or not the swallows might also survive." He looked at them triumphantly. "Perhaps by changing their diet."

"As the owl suggested," said Wake.

The blue tit did not seem grateful for this reminder. "That was theory, this is practice. There's all the difference in the world."

To appreciate the considerable dismay caused among the swallows by the blue tit's suggestion you have to understand something of the way birds feel about food. They are very finicky, as the saying goes. Birds of different species eat different things.[5] Their food is so different that they even have beaks of different shapes to eat it with. It's just not done for birds of one species to eat the sort of food enjoyed by birds of another species.

So strongly do birds feel about this matter that it is considered extremely impolite for one species to discuss the eating habits of another. And here was the blue tit suggesting a CHANGE OF DIET.

The blue tit had clearly been busy. For the next hour or so the swallows watched with growing astonishment from the branches of a pear tree as one of the most extraordinary scenes the forest had ever seen took place below them, on the grass under the orchard trees.

I am sure that many of you have been to church on the morning of Harvest Sunday. You have seen the fruit and vegetables, washed and polished and carefully arranged in silver dishes and dark straw baskets, laid out at the front of the church in the dim light entering through the coloured windows as though for a mysterious feast. The scene under the pear tree was something like that, for it was there that the blue tit was staging what amounted to the very first harvest festival of the birds. (Since food is so uncertain for the birds during the winter I am surprised no one had thought of it before.)

The first birds to fly down into the damp orchard garden were the other members of the tit family. There were blue tits, coal tits and great tits. In old Icelandic the word "tittr" actually meant a small bird and the tits were indeed very small but clamped in each tiny beak was a single berry or a few seeds. "Down there," the blue

---

[5] *If you find it strange that birds do not enjoy each other's food let me remind you how many times you have pushed something to the side of your plate while eating school dinners only to have some fattish boy or girl lean over with gleaming eyes and say: "If you don't want that cabbage and/or semolina I'll have it." In short, if there are so many varied human responses to cabbage and/or semolina why should birds be any different?*

38

tit commanded and the visitors emptied their beaks into one of the large dock leaves which had been arranged in a line under the trees. Next to arrive were two blackbirds. They brought hawthorn berries and a large protesting worm which they also deposited on one of the large leaves before volunteering to keep watch.

"If anyone comes near we will sing," they proclaimed but it was soon apparent that this was a most impractical suggestion. Just as the birds were starting to arrive in considerable numbers with their offerings of food the clear musical notes of the blackbirds' song were suddenly heard sounding what everyone assumed to be a warning and in a flash the garden emptied. It had been a false alarm caused by the total inability of the blackbirds to control their tendency to sing without warning.

"Sorry," they cried, as the birds which had panicked at the sound returned rather sheepishly to the orchard. "We forgot".

Twice more this happened before the blue tit abandoned any pretence of patience and irritably instructed the blackbirds to follow a different course. They would now sing continuously and stop only if an intruder appeared. This proved to be a much better idea, with the blackbirds providing some rather pleasant background music, as the birds continued to arrive with their offerings; whether or not the blackbirds would have been prepared to stop singing in the event of an emergency was happily never put to the test.

Every few minutes now birds were arriving with their offerings. The sparrows brought seeds; the robins brought caterpillars and beetles; the thrushes came with berries and small snails. Some of the visitors had seldom if ever been so far inland before. Down in the orchard the birds heard a sad, sea sound coming from the direction of the estuary and two curlews flew in with small crabs and cockles. Even the black-headed gulls Wake had first met at the end of the summer had learned what was happening; one of them alighted with a tiny silvery fish. The rooks arrived with empty beaks, apologising profusely. "We were bringing some food but we became hungry without warning on the way over and accidentally swallowed it. We can go back if you like."

The blue tit waved them away in exasperation and the rooks flew to a nearby branch where they proceeded to discuss what was happening in very loud voices, in order to be heard above the song of the blackbirds who glared at them from opposite ends of the orchard, unable to stop singing and rebuke them, in case this provoked another panic. Altogether it was a rather chaotic scene but the blue tit at last seemed satisfied and called for silence.

"We will now"--

And then the blue tit stopped. His eyes widened in astonishment. The others turned and followed his gaze. One or two of them gasped. The blackbirds ceased to sing. The rooks stopped chattering. Bess edged a little closer to Wake and there was even a possibility that he edged a little closer to her. They all stared transfixed towards the far end of the orchard and the object hurtling towards them, skimming in low under the trees. Wings beat lazily; there was a face as round as a moon, jovial, terrible, and yet oddly unfinished; and a shape so big that it completely filled the aisle beneath the branches. With a final enormous flap of its great wings the hurtling shape alighted on the grass and to their great relief the birds saw it had materialised into something familiar.

The owl smiled grimly as he perceived the stunned silence. "As we arranged I have myself brought a small sample." One or two of the other birds shivered slightly as they noticed something small and sad which had dropped from his curved beak and was lying at his feet. Just about the same size as a swallow, thought Wake.

As might have been expected the blue tit was the first to recover his composure. "You're last," he observed and then he looked across at the owl and added rather nervously: "So far, of course."

All the different samples of food were now laid out in two roughly straight lines, across the grass beneath the trees. The birds who had brought the food waited a little anxiously beside each sample. More from politeness than anything else one or two of them were pretending to admire each other's offerings.

The blue tit who seemed to spend his life calling for silence did so again. "Now remember this is a very serious occasion and there isn't a lot of time. We are trying to see if the swallows could exist on any of the foods you have brought here this morning. It may well be that they could not, but we will at least have established that fact.

"The swallows will now pass among you, as you explain what the food is and where it is obtained and any other relevant information; unusual recipes, meals for special occasions, economy dishes, that sort of thing." He looked across at the owl who was perched on a branch a few feet away, regarding the other birds with an expression on his face which suggested that he was discreetly appraising them in terms of taste and tenderness. "We'll start with the owl who I'm sure is anxious to get away."

The owl had clearly been expecting nothing less. "Thank you," he began. "I had thought of delivering a short address illustrating the dietary habits of the owl; its surprising variety; vitamin and fibre content; absence of harmful additives; that sort of thing. In the end I came to the conclusion that most of it would have been over your heads."

He paused, apparently sensing that the other birds were reserving most of their attention not for him but for the object lying at his feet. "So instead I decided that if the swallows were going to spend the winter with us we ought to make their stay as memorable as possible and so I have brought along what is for us a rather rare delicacy."

"What is it, owl?" demanded a rook admiringly, hopping along the branch for a closer look.

"It's a small mammal or rodent. I won't burden you with its scientific name, rook. It's all in Latin which I don't believe you're acquainted with. As I say it's a great delicacy and the swallows are welcome to sample a portion; a small portion."

This time it was the gull who interrupted. "It's funny you should say that because we gulls regard this fish as a very special delicacy also." He smiled thinly at the owl. "With the added advantage that it has no fur, so there's no waste." He looked up affectionately at the swallows. "Nothing but the best for my friend, Wake."

That really was the main problem. All the birds had brought along the foods they reserved for special occasions. They meant well; no one can deny it. People usually do mean well when they serve up a rare delicacy. But as you know yourselves there are those who consider that the most attractive feature of a rare delicacy is its rarity. Such people are inclined to scowl down at the plate and say: "What is it?" turning it over experimentally with a fork, to demonstrate to fascinated onlookers that it is even worse underneath. When they find themselves staring down at things like oysters, snails, frogs' legs, caviar, or even in some cases sprouts, such people are often quite relieved to learn that they are in short supply and in some cases practically unobtainable and if anyone suggests trying to obtain some more, on some future occasion, they tend to say: "Please don't bother on my account. An experience so enchanting should never be coarsened by familiarity." I myself have never really seen the point of food from which you are obliged to avert your eyes.

As I say it would have been bad enough if the birds had simply brought along examples of their ordinary, everyday foods, but by bringing their "rare delicacies" they had ensured that the experiment failed. It was not only the swallows who found the foods presented by the other birds completely uneatable; all those assembled in the orchard seemed to feel the same way. They were, of course, enormously polite, especially if invited to try a taste.

"It looks very nice," they assured each other," but I've just had breakfast."

"Not just now," they protested. "Don't want to spoil my lunch."

"Awfully sorry," they apologised, "but I'm trying to lose a bit of weight."

Discussion of food is always painful to those in the unfortunate position of being edible so the worm decided to take advantage of this temporary lull in eating to wriggle over the edge of the grass and disappear under the earth. No one bothered to alert the blackbird who was in any case pre-occupied with fending off some crabmeat proffered rather persistently by the gull. In the end, to the blackbird's enormous relief, the gull polished it off himself, as he had not yet had breakfast. From a safe distance everyone admired the owl's furry delicacy but insisted that they wouldn't dream of depriving him of it.

Wake saw that it was hopeless. The resident birds would rather go hungry than eat each other's foods and the swallows were the same. It was now clear to him that migrant birds flew south in the winter because there was no alternative; they could leave or they could starve to death. This was their destiny and had been since the very first swallows.

He gazed down at the birds milling about on the grass of the orchard in the thin winter sunlight. Already they seemed to have forgotten why they were there. For them this had probably been no more than a social occasion, a little diversion before winter began confining them more and more to their home territories, making such gatherings impossible. He could not really blame them. How could they be expected to understand the plight of the swallows? Very soon, as winter tightened its grip on the land, they would have their own problems.

As he looked down, though, Wake found his own feelings

slowly changing. At first there had been merely disappointment at the failure of the experiment but now he was starting to feel just a little angry. He had been wasting time. Ever since the swallows had found themselves alone in this wintry landscape all he had done was listen to others, resident birds who knew nothing of the way the swallows lived. These birds chattering away so amiably together down there beneath him never went anywhere. What could a thrush know of the mountains? What could a blackbird know of the sea? And the owl who flew in a darkness as bright as day; could he also fly in darkness all through the night and still be flying when the morning came? He had wasted enough time. The swallows must now start to take responsibility for themselves. He looked along the branch of the pear tree at his five companions. It was time to end the confusion and uncertainty he sensed in them; time to put his own idea to the test. The fact that it was yet another idea based on something the owl had said did not necessarily mean that it was unworkable.

In later years some of those who were present in the orchard would try to create a bit of a stir by claiming that they had actually heard the famous remark which Wake now made; they were mistaken, for he murmured those momentous words and only the blue tit and the swallows were close enough to hear them. Turning to his companions, he said: "I have had enough of this. It is time for us to go. There is much to be done. We have to prepare for Africa.".

With that Wake thanked the blue tit for his trouble and the swallows rose from the branch of the old pear tree and disappeared, heading back towards the barn and of all the resident birds still milling about on the grass under the orchard trees only the blue tit watched them go and his eyes were thoughtful.

Wake flew home with his companions, feeling curiously relieved. Ever since the main group had left (how long ago it all seemed now) one image had haunted his thoughts; it was the image of Creakwing all alone in this bare, cold land with all the swallows gone. Now he knew what had to be done, or rather what had to be attempted and even if they failed Creakwing would at least be part of it and they would all perish together. As they returned he was too deep in thought to notice that for the first time he was at the front and all the other swallows were flying behind him.

His new-found resolution became even stronger when they arrived back at the barn and he discovered why Creakwing had not attended the demonstration in the orchard. The swallows were now all living together, occupying the nests in the barn where Wake had once lived with his family. Being together made it easier for them to talk things over and it was especially pleasant to be able to talk things over, as loudly as possible, in the evenings when the light faded early and they realised once again that nowhere in the darkness all around them were there any other swallows.

It was still early afternoon but already getting dark when they arrived back and flew in through the hole near the rafters. They could not see Creakwing but his voice greeted them from the gloom at the rear of the barn.

"Sorry I couldn't make it to your little experiment." His voice was bright and cheerful. "I'm afraid this old wing of mine finally seems to have given up. I intended looking for some food this afternoon but I couldn't even get out of the barn."

Don't worry, Wake thought. You won't have to fly anywhere. If my plan succeeds you will make the most comfortable Crossing in the history of the swallows. At that stage he decided to say nothing about his intentions; Creakwing might be infirm but he was still their leader and Wake did not want to be ordered to abandon his plan; he would hate to have to defy such a respected swallow!

Even so the old leader insisted on being told exactly what had happened in the orchard during the blue tit's experiment. Once or twice he shook his head over some specially foolish aspect of the occasion, but he made no further criticism of what had happened, even when Wake concluded by saying that the whole morning had been a total waste of time. "Particularly when time is the one thing we can't afford to waste."

It was impossible to tell if Creakwing had hoped for anything from the demonstration. He merely said: "So now you will be leaving, I trust? You do understand, I hope, that you must go now?"

Wake regarded his leader through eyes which were clear and candid. "We will be leaving within the next few days," he said.

It was almost dark when Wake set off a few hours later on the most important mission of his life. He was quite alone, on a journey which took him deeper and deeper into the forest. He could not suppress a little shiver as he sensed the dark shapes closing round him. Where once the trees had formed a tossing canopy of green, filled with secret places where the birds could hide and sing, they were now gaunt and still and leaves as dark as blood dripped down through the gloom and on to the soft and rotting forest floor.

He was away from the barn for a very long time. He was away for so long that when he returned the other swallows experienced that most curious mixture of emotions we feel when we are both angry with someone for staying away and relieved to see them return. Even more frustratingly he refused to explain where he had been. With a contented smile he urged them to be patient. "Go to sleep now. Tomorrow I will tell you everything. After all, you are all part of the plan." The swallows looked solemn and important, as befits those who are part of a plan, and questioned him no further.

When they were all asleep Wake flew up to an opening in the roof of the barn. The night was clear and the sky was full of stars and as he gazed upwards it seemed as though all at once the sky turned over. Now the stars were below and he was gazing down on *them*. It was an effort for him to hold his gaze on that stupendous sight for the stars both frightened and bewildered him. They seemed to be enticing him, urging him to leap down and be lost among them. How could there be a pathway to Africa through all that bright wilderness ?

He found himself thinking of his mother. Once, in that very place, he had been able to lie in his nest knowing she was there beside him in the darkness. What was she doing at that very moment? Was she thinking of him? If she was thinking of him he hoped she was remembering the few nice things he had said and done and not the other things.

Alone under the stars, anxious not to disturb his sleeping comrades, he whispered: "We are coming, mother. And Creakwing will be with us."

* * *

45

In later years a great debate was to rage among the more scholarly swallows about precisely when Wake had his Great Idea. They quarrelled about it whenever it was mentioned. They even came to blows about it, although fortunately they were only token blows, from one respected scholar to another and no one was hurt. More serious was the fact that at least two elderly swallows refused to speak to each other for years after falling out over the matter and long after they had made it up their descendants were still vigorously pursuing the dispute on the grounds that it was affording far too much innocent pleasure to be abandoned.

Those involved in the argument seemed to fall into two main groups. There was the school of thought which argued for a single blinding flash of inspiration. This was known as the Big Bang theory and those swallows which supported it argued that Wake simply looked down on the resident birds on the morning of the blue tit's little experiment in the orchard and realised in an instant what had to be done.

The other group argued that it had been a gradual process, an idea which grew and developed in Wake's mind over many weeks. This was known as the Steady State theory. The birds which supported this idea went right back to the beginning, to the late summer when Wake had first seen the large orange handkerchief with the bright yellow sun in the centre. They quoted verbatim the owl's helpful reference to the possibility of a resident bird carrying Creakwing to Africa and spending the winter there. And mentioned in passing the small mammal or rodent which Wake had observed him carry down to the orchard.

If the scholar birds were interested only in the prospect of a good old academic brawl the bardic birds were interested only in having a good tune with good words to sing to it. If ever they found the facts of a swallow legend to be true but dull, it was their practice to create some new and more appealing facts which fitted the music better. Their account of the Winter Crossing extended to some 24 verses and was performed only if five or more swallows specially requested it, although by the end of such performances, through a mixture of guilt and cowardice, it usually proved impossible to identify the culprits who had asked for it. The bardic version told how a long-dead hero most of the swallows had never heard of appeared to Wake in a vision, perched on a shimmering golden telephone wire, and in awesome tones, using words like "Behold" and "Beware", instructed him in what he must do. This bardic version, being more interesting, was the one which was generally accepted.

No one thought to ask Wake until it was too late, because by that time he was far too important and distinguished to be bothered with such a minor inquiry. In any case I happen to know (don't ask me how, but we authors have our sources) that if they had asked him Wake would have been obliged to say that he did not know where the idea came from; it simply appeared without warning. This seems reasonable to me; if we knew where good ideas were kept we could go and get them whenever we wanted and the world would be a much more sensible place.

I am happy to say that there is no dispute at all about who was first to hear what Wake intended to do. When he left the other swallows to fly deep into the forest on the evening of the blue tit's experiment he was on his way to see a group of birds he had never met before, a group of birds with very special skills.

He had seen the jackdaws many times. Indeed they were so sociable and friendly that it was difficult not to notice them. They went everywhere together and loved to mingle with other birds, especially when feeding in the morning and at night. And yet there was something mysterious about them. The jackdaws dwelt in the depths of the forest because they had many secrets; things they did not wish to be known and objects they did not wish to be seen. The curious thing was that although the birds all knew this and shunned a place where they were clearly not welcome the jackdaws themselves were mainly concerned to keep their secrets from Man who had long been the victim of their strange ways.

Wake had never before called on the jackdaws at home, nor had he ever heard of any other swallow doing so, especially not at night. He was not even certain how to find them. All he knew was that they were said to live alone in the middle of the forest, far from the haunts of any other birds, in a place deserted even by its human inhabitants long ago. Several times during the journey he lost his bearings and had to stop, baffled by the darkness and the way all the trees looked the same.

At last, just when he was starting to think that perhaps the jackdaws did not even live in the forest, he saw to his relief that the trees were thinning out and he found himself flying into a clearing. It was the place he had been looking for. Warily he alighted on a branch at the edge of the clearing and remained absolutely still as he waited to see if anyone had noticed his arrival.

The clearing lay before him, still and silent, bathed in the ornamental light of a dome of glittering stars and a big yellow moon. Every detail could be seen. The darker shape in the centre of the clearing was the ruins of a cottage. Enormous blocks of stone from its walls, stained green by the passage of the years, lay tumbled in the long grass. Stout oak beams had fallen from the roof and now lay rotting inside the crumbling walls. Several large trees had also taken root inside the ruin and with the passage of time their branches had spread out to occupy the rooms where once long ago people had lived.

Re-assured by the silence, Wake flitted across the clearing and perched on the rotting wooden lintel of one of the cottage windows, wondering what to do next. At first he could not tell where the noise was coming from. There seemed to be two distinct sounds. There was a faint clinking as though things made of metal were being scraped together. The other sound came in brief bursts and made him shiver slightly, because it sounded very much like laughter, raucous, cackling laughter. The worrying thing was that the sounds seemed to be coming from somewhere quite close although when he looked around nothing stirred anywhere in the moonlit clearing. He listened more carefully and was astonished to realise that the sounds must be coming from the very building on which he was perched. At the far end of the abandoned cottage a small section of roof was still intact and at the top there was a large chimney with a pot on top. Whoever was making the sounds appeared to be inside it!

Uneasily, Wake cleared his throat and called out a rather discreet "Hello" in the faint hope that those inside might be a little hard of hearing but the response was instantaneous. First he heard a loud oath.[6] This was followed by a muffled crash, as though something

_____

[6] *Some very careful research has established that the expression used by the jackdaw was one of those oaths which are all the more effective for containing the element of surprise, since apparently none of his companions was even aware that he knew the word! This often happens with people, too.*

had been dropped rather hurriedly. Then four dark and glittering eyes were regarding him over the rim of the chimney pot.

Throughout his journey into the forest Wake had been endlessly repeating to himself the things he intended to say but now his mind was empty. He could only stare back at the two dark shapes confronting him from the rim of the chimney. Those glittering eyes turned away from him and swept around the moonlit glade and then apparently satisfied that he was alone the two birds hopped out on to the rim of the chimney. It was the smaller of the two jackdaws which broke the silence

"We have a visitor, dear." Her eyes never left his face. "Isn't that nice?"

They were like two dark shadows on the night. And they were not alone. From all over the ruins he could hear soft whispers, the flutter of wings.

"How clever of you to find us," said the lady jackdaw. "But you really can't expect us to invite you in when you arrive without warning, at such a late hour. As a matter of fact we were planning an early night, just as soon as we've finished polishing-----"

At these words her partner lazily unfolded one enormous wing and draped it across her face and beak in a symbolic gesture with which she was evidently very familiar, for she stopped talking immediately and continued to scrutinise him in silence, with a smile of such sinister understanding that Wake was quite relieved when the other jackdaw took up the conversation.

"I am convinced it is a swallow," he said. "A swallow come to visit us in the middle of the night and almost in the middle of winter. What can it all mean?" Here he raised his voice as though seeking an answer from the rustling shadows but a soft excited whispering was the only response. His voice sank to a sly murmur. "What are you doing here boy? Who sent you. And why aren't you in Africa?"

Wake felt confused by all the questions; confused and frightened. By now a nice friendly conversation should have been taking place, with perhaps a little joke here and there and the odd exclamation of: "Really?" Instead he was under interrogation from two very unfriendly jackdaws who seemed able to see him a great more clearly than he could see them, in the presence of an equally invisible audience, all whispering together in a distinctly secretive manner. He completely forgot his intention of revealing the purpose of his visit in a discreet and tactful way.

"I was just wondering," he said, "if you could possibly find time to steal something for me."

It sounded even worse out loud than it had sounded in his head and this was confirmed by the reaction of the lady jackdaw who seemed more stricken by his words than he had ever thought possible.

"Oh the shame of it," she wailed, hopping around the rim of the chimney pot until she had completely turned her back on him. Her shoulders shook tragically. "Once more we are to be accused. Will it never end? A few little trinkets here and there, the merest trifles chosen for their pretty colours and the world calls us thieves. It is too cruel."

Completely taken aback by this outburst, Wake could feel only gratitude when the other jackdaw hopped around the chimney top to his partner's side and once more unfurled his great wing to tenderly veil those anguished features. The lady jackdaw's wild lamentations were instantly extinguished.

"As you see, boy, your words have wounded an innocent heart. What do you mean 'steal'?"

Every instinct was telling him to flee; to mumble some apology about having made a terrible mistake and leave. He was alone in the night and far from home and surrounded by these most sinister jackdaws who seemed quite different from the birds he had observed so often in the daylight. He had also somehow offended them. And yet he could not move. Even if he fled now he would have to return. Too much was at stake.

"I am deeply sorry if I have offended and upset your wife," he said sincerely. "I am very young and sometimes I do not say exactly what I mean. I meant to say that the jackdaws are famous among birds for their very special skills and I need those skills. I need them very badly." Both jackdaws were listening intently. "I need them to save the life of our leader, Creakwing."

The female jackdaw gave a little sniff to remind him of her recent grief while her partner regarded him thoughtfully from the rim of the chimney. "You, if I am not mistaken, are Wake, the famous swallow?" Wake nodded with just a hint of defiance. "Well, my little friend, you have made a common mistake which is easily understandable; to steal is to take something of value, with the intention of permanently depriving the owner of possession. That is the law; you can take it from me. And although it is true to say we jackdaws do occasionally acquire things we do so not because they are of value but because they are beautiful. And who is to say it is not our intention one day to give them back? Can we really call that stealing?"

"Men call you the Prince of Thieves," Wake reminded him.[7]

"The Prince of Collectors would be kinder," said the jackdaw. "We collect things."

During this exchange Wake did not notice the lady jackdaw hop down from the chimney. Now he heard her calling his name from the shadows. "Come and see." He hesitated and her voice came again, softly beseeching him through the silvery darkness of the moonlit roof. "Come and see my pretty things."

Again he hesitated. Was it a trap of some kind? Why should the jackdaws allow him to share their secrets if there was a chance that he might speak of what he had seen?

"Go on," the other jackdaw encouraged. His voice was not unfriendly. "And then you will describe for us the pretty thing which you desire."

He found the lady jackdaw perched on the rim of a different chimney, a larger one at the back of the roof, and alighted there beside her. For a moment her closeness made him tremble. She was easily eight times bigger than he was and her towering shape shimmered and gleamed from head to foot like dark waters falling in the night.

"Look down," she commanded softly.

At first, as he gazed down, he could see nothing and then deep inside the chimney something began to stir. The interior began to brighten. Colours appeared, greens and golds and reds and yellows and blues. The effect was coming from countless coloured objects carefully arranged inside the chimney, trinkets of every kind, strewn across the floor and attached to the sides of the jackdaw's rickety nest so that every single surface was covered by them; glittering colours, all jostling together, as though competing for his attention. Like the flames of a furnace they flickered there below him and just for a moment he found himself wondering what would

---

[7] *"The Jackdaw of Rheims", about a thieving jackdaw who stole the ring of the Cardinal Archbishop of Rheims, is the best-known poem on the subject. In that case, to the jackdaw's eternal credit, the ring was returned.*

happen if he was to lose his balance and fall down into that roaring brightness.

"Is it as fine as these?" the lady jackdaw murmured at his ear. "Is the thing you must possess as rare as these?"

The male jackdaw had now joined them. "This is our finest collection," he explained with gruff pride. "We only show it to those who seem really interested." He smiled confidentially. "I would ask you, of course, not to........"

"Of course," Wake assured him. "I will never mention what I have seen. And I can now see why the jackdaws are such renowned.... collectors."

"Quite so," agreed the jackdaw, "but now you must tell us why you are here and what you want of us."

It is extremely difficult, of course, to confront another bird with any sort of confidence when you are obliged to lean back and look up at it from what seems at the time like a long way below but Wake did his best. He began by reminding the two jackdaws of the great fame they enjoyed among other birds. He was encouraged to observe that neither appeared to find any fault with this suggestion and there was even a low murmur of approbation from the shadows and one those of those solitary shouts which can be so embarrassing, as one of the jackdaws said: "Bravo" and immediately regretted it.

The jackdaws, Wake suggested, were unique in the forest. No man knew their secrets and yet they moved freely through the world of Man, stealing whatever bright trinket took their fancy wherever it might be. Both jackdaws winced slightly at this slip of the tongue but seemed hesitant to interrupt so perceptive a speech.

"I have come here," he concluded, "to ask you to take something from Man for me."

"Collect," corrected the larger jackdaw mildly.

"I want you to collect something belonging to Man which will save Creakwing's life."

"And what is this rare and wonderful object?"

Wake glanced at the lady jackdaw and said deprecatingly: "It is certainly not as fine as the things in your collection." She nodded graciously. "It is... a handkerchief."

The lady jackdaw snorted in derision but ventured no further comment as her partner's great wing appeared ominously overhead. In any case she was clearly too fascinated to interrupt.

"Where is this handkerchief?"

"It is at the farm."

"Whereabouts at the farm?"

"Inside"

"Whereabouts inside?"

"I don't know."

In the thoughtful silence which now settled on the group Wake found himself wondering how it could be that an idea which seemed perfectly substantial when it was only in your head could seem so small and incomplete when you mentioned it to someone else. He had the strong impression that the two jackdaws were too astonished to speak and even the whispering and the rustling in the darkness all around him had ceased, as the whole colony of jackdaws awaited his next observation, in a mood, he realised uncomfortably, which had suddenly turned to awe, with just a suggestion of dread. The larger jackdaw recovered his composure first.

"Why do you ask the jackdaws to risk their lives to obtain this handkerchief? What miraculous properties does it possess that you are willing to ask us to die for it?"

Those solemn words were precisely what Wake needed to remove any impression there might be that he was not himself aware of the true significance of his request.

"If you agree to risk your lives to help us and take this handkerchief from inside the farm I will use it to save Creakwing's life. It is as important as that."

One of the really nice moments in life is when you finally reveal some fine intention you have been absolutely dying to talk about and everyone says: "Really?.. how marvellous... Do you mean it?.. You're not having me on?.. how super. .just fancy.. wait 'til I tell the others." Wake felt a little bit like that as he outlined his plan. It was the first time he had told anyone about it. He anticipated that the idea would be greeted with admiration and a great many eager questions. Fears would be expressed for his safety and it would probably be suggested that he was a little too daring for his own good. He was not basically vain but these after all were his secret thoughts and I suspect that most of us are secretly a good deal vainer than we would ever be prepared to confess. He was to be disappointed.

"The very idea," said the lady jackdaw when he had concluded his explanation. "Why don't you take me as well? I've never been to Africa"

Wake was not familiar with sarcasm. "I don't think we could manage both of you," he said. The lady jackdaw who was inclined to fret about her weight pursed her beak at the implications of this remark but said nothing further, as laughter was suppressed in the darkness all around her.

It was her partner, however, who made him feel much more nervous. He was not interested in the honour and the glory involved in Wake's great idea; he demanded the details of the plan. He wanted to know what would happen first and what would happen last and all the little moments in between, arranged in the correct order. These were things Wake had not really thought about. Like a glorious banner, the great plan had unfurled across his mind devoid of detail, but in his confusion he stumbled upon the only answer which could not be contradicted. "I don't know," he kept repeating, over and over, until the jackdaw finally tired of attempting to reveal some facts which he could denounce.

Unnoticed in the darkness, other jackdaws had appeared on the roof all around them and were listening intently.

"Why does he have to have this handkerchief and no other?" a voice inquired.

"Doesn't he realise it could be absolutely anywhere?" complained another.

"Has he ever been inside a house himself?" demanded a third.

Each inquiry brought the same response from the lady jackdaw. "Exactly," she said grimly and glared at the little swallow as though she had disliked him for years. Perhaps it was this general hostility which made the jackdaw leader's manner a little more sympathetic.

"Does Creakwing know about all this?" he inquired mildly. This shook Wake a little. He had been giving a great deal of thought himself to the best way of informing the swallows' leader of the plan and to what he would do if Creakwing refused to agree to it.

"He doesn't know yet," he said. "But if there is no other way I think he will come."

"But there is another way," the jackdaw corrected, with an air of deep regret. "A way which Creakwing fully understands. You can leave without him. I am sure that is what he has told you to do."

The jackdaws awaited his response. It was clear that they had now dismissed any idea of taking part in the exploit he had proposed; they were much more relaxed as they awaited confirmation that he had withdrawn his wild request.

Now, clearly, was the time to move on to conversation a good deal lighter and more agreeable in character, possibly concerned with the pastime of collecting things. As he looked around the circle of jackdaws Wake could not help feeling just a little bit trapped but his voice was calm and courteous.

"Thank you for listening to me," he said, sensing the silence of anticipation all around him. "I came here to ask for your help because everyone knows of your great reputation. I should have known, perhaps, that you did not care about the possibility of further fame. Now I must get help from somewhere else."

The leader of the jackdaws looked just a little uncomfortable. "We declined to take the handkerchief from inside the farm because it is too dangerous. Why should any other birds take a different view?"

"I know that nothing like this has ever been attempted before," Wake agreed, "but that is exactly why I believe another group of birds might just decide to help. The ones I am thinking of are not as famous as you now but if they succeed I am sure they will be afterwards."

The two jackdaws perched on the rim of the chimney turned sideways to contemplate each other with dawning dismay, as they sensed a small and unguarded portal silently opening to admit a new and furtive possibility.

"Which birds?" inquired the male jackdaw casually.

"If you refuse to steal the handkerchief from the farm," said Wake, "I believe I might be able to persuade the magpies [8] to help. Perhaps they're not as skilful as the jackdaws but then again they may be more daring. Especially if they feel that by helping the swallows they will become even more famous. We shall have to see."

Discreet but widespread consternation now ensued. The female jackdaw snorted haughtily. All around him in the ruins dismayed

---

[8] *The magpies, too, were famous thieves; the most celebrated being the hero of the opera "The Thieving Magpie" by Rossini. Personally, I could never be close friends with a bird which goes around apparently trailing a long, dark cloak.*

jackdaws hopped forward out of the concealing shadows, so that he could see them clearly for the first time. Their leader held up his enormous wing for silence.

"I am sure we are all agreed that we cannot allow this plan to fail by entrusting it to the magpies." There were murmurs of agreement at this and one of the jackdaws was moved to remark that it was "cheek" on the part of the magpies even to consider receiving such an invitation.

The jackdaw turned back to Wake. "We do not approve of your plan. We believe it will fail and that you would be well-advised to leave without Creakwing but if by any chance this business is going to become celebrated it would be a pity to spoil it all by involving the magpies." He glanced down fondly at his partner. "In any case I believe you, my dear, have never actually been inside a house before."

"I've been inside on window ledges," she reminded him.

"Not quite the same thing, though, I don't think."

So she was to be the one? Somehow he had assumed that it would be her partner. Wake saw that the substantial air of testiness had vanished from the female jackdaw's face and her dark eyes were shining with a strange new excitement.

"That's settled then," said the leader of the jackdaws." There is no time to lose. We will meet you outside the farmhouse at dawn tomorrow." His glance held that of the little swallow. "As for you my young friend, I do hope I can assume that you are already starting to forget the things you have seen here tonight."......

As he returned to the barn a new anxiety was absorbing all Wake's thoughts. His plan was now well-advanced; he had sought and obtained the assistance of the jackdaws; the time had come to act. And yet Creakwing still knew nothing of his plan and might possibly instruct him to abandon it. What troubled him was the thought that he was not absolutely sure he could obey such an order.

He need not have worried. During the night Creakwing's injury became much worse. By the gloomy morning light they saw that his wing was stiff and swollen. If anything brushed against it he sucked in his breath and closed his eyes in a thoughtful sort of way. He shivered constantly but even more worrying were the things he said. The rain pattered across the roof of the barn with each surge of the wind. Down below them lengths of timber stacked on the floor rattled continuously in the icy blast and yet Creakwing seemed to think it was still late summer, with the Crossing about to begin. He kept repeating their instructions over and over again but his voice was soft and dreamy and his eyes did not seem to see them. It proved impossible to tell him anything.

To avoid disturbing him, Wake whispered the outline of his plan to the others, in a voice hoarse with suppressed excitement. For a moment he was made to feel quite uneasy by their response, for when he finished speaking there was absolute silence; he was convinced they disapproved and then at last they responded.

Oliver spoke first, his voice grave and momentous.

"I always knew," he said, "that one day we would all be celebrated heroes with our own fame names and songs sung about us."

"I, of course, will fly at the front to watch out for dangers ahead," announced Bony.

"And I'll be at the back, to guard against the dangers behind," said Harold, puzzlingly.

Bess was her usual gentle and sensible self. "I'll watch over Creakwing and see that he is comfortable. He is probably going to be very nervous."

None of them seemed to have any doubts about the wisdom of the plan. To tell the truth they had become very bored, sitting around all day, waiting for something to happen, deeply puzzled and even inclined to exchange meaningful glances in front of him, over his frequent and mysterious excursions from the barn. All this time their only instruction from Creakwing had been to try to put on weight and in the whole world there is no activity less exciting than steadily growing fatter. Now, though, they were gloriously in his confidence and part of these high and heroic intentions. Once more, despite the gravity of their plight, it was fun to be a swallow.

Reflecting on the enormous size of the jackdaws, their glittering eyes and their fierce way of talking to swallows, Wake had become convinced that meeting them might be an interesting experience for Bess, so he decided to take her along with him when he set out for his meeting at the farmhouse.

It was already light when they arrived and the jackdaws had got there before them. There were three of them, the two birds he had talked to the previous night and another he did not recognise. They were lined up on the bare branch of a tree commanding a good view straight across the lawn, with its litter of damp brown leaves, to the back of the building and the kitchen door, the very lawn on which he had watched the old man lying in his chair in the sun so long ago. But it was many days since the old man had been able to take his ease in the sheltered warmth of the garden and the door was now firmly closed.

Wake could not help noticing that Bess also seemed a little nervous in such close proximity to three large jackdaws, so he edged along the branch as though he had known them for years and inquired in a comradely sort of way about the plan.

"Mind where you're putting your feet," said the jackdaw's leader. Wake looked down and saw for the first time, alongside the jackdaw, on the branch, secured around a slight protuberance in the bark, a large ruby ring glittering in the early morning light. He presumed it had come from the collection he had inspected the night before but what on earth was it doing there beside the jackdaws? They did not seem in a mood to explain so he did not ask.

To his relief the lady jackdaw did not seem nearly so irritable as she had been the night before. She was studying the back of the farmhouse, her eyes alert and yet calm. Wake followed her gaze and subjected the rear window and the door of the farmhouse to the same determined scrutiny, although not completely sure what he was being so determined about, since nothing at all seemed to be happening.

"That's the room we are interested in," the lady jackdaw murmured, almost to herself. "There's an old armchair in there where the old man likes to take a nap in the winter when it's too cold to sit outside. Luckily for you we've been watching this house for years."

"In fact," said her partner, "it is said that we have been taking things from this particular house since the very first year it was occupied. It's the sort of tradition we jackdaws are rather proud of."

The lady jackdaw looked at Wake for the first time. "It was fortunate you came to see us when you did. If we are not mistaken this is the day when they like to come outside to hang their collection of clothes in the garden for everyone to see. Why they should bother to collect clothes is quite beyond me but at least it means the door will have to remain open for a little while." She paused and then added mildly: "He could be a problem, though."

Wake studied the back of the farmhouse with great care but failed to identify anything even vaguely resembling a problem. "Who?" he inquired.

"Look in the corner of the big window. Can you see him? He can certainly see you."

Wake followed her gaze. The window was long and jutted out from the wall so that it overhung the garden. Inside, the space between the curtains and the window formed a little alcove and in this space he now observed a cage hanging down from the ceiling by a long brass chain. Inside it, clinging to the bars on the side nearest to the window and gazing out intently into the garden was a tiny yellow bird.

"He's been watching us ever since we arrived. He knows there's something going on."

Wake had never seen a bird locked up in a cage before. He had not known that such things happened. To have to live inside a cage inside a house was bad enough but to have to do so when you had wings and could fly seemed to him the saddest thing he could possibly imagine. He wondered if their appearance in the garden was making the little prisoner unhappy by reminding him of what it was like to be free. Out in the open on that winter morning, shivering and hungry, Wake could feel only pity for the little yellow bird in its situation of warmth and comfort.

The lady jackdaw seemed almost amused by this complication. "He is a very fine fellow, no mistake about that. He makes me feel positively dowdy but what I would like to know from that pretty little thing is exactly whose side he is on. However, I rather feel we will have to wait and see." All at once she snapped out of this mood of gentle reverie.

"Right, the first thing we have to do is hide you and your little friend. It is generally assumed that all the swallows have left here long ago and if you're seen it won't be long before those rude people with glasses [9] start to arrive to see why you're stuck here in a

---

[9] *I must say I have never thought of bird watching as being rude but it does make you think, doesn't it? All I can suggest is that if you are studying a bird and it starts to do something you suspect it would be mortified to discover you were observing you might consider pretending to clean your binoculars, while coughing discreetly, to give it time to recover its composure*

tree at the beginning of winter, instead of warm and cosy in Africa." She pointed towards the back of the farmhouse. "Get up there if you want to stay."

You have probably noticed that a very old house looks as though it has always been there. It's hard to believe that once it must have been new, smelling of paint and wood and that one day the men building it stepped back, looked up, grinned and said: "Finished at last. Now for a big mug of tea." The farmhouse was that sort of place. You could tell it had been built a long time ago because to make the walls the workmen had used huge stones, all of different sizes but so snugly fitted together that it seemed as though they were growing there.

Over the years these ancient walls had slowly become hidden under a thick curtain of green. The trees growing up the walls were very old. Close to the ground their branches were thick and strong but higher up slender and supple and here in the summer it was their custom to pause briefly in their upward striving, to flower and loll about in the warmth of the sun; all except one, because the ivy never flowered and never rested. Always it climbed steadily upwards as though some mysterious appointment awaited it right at the very top.

On still summer days this soaring wilderness was constantly twitching with the movements of tiny creatures hardly ever seen. Bees wandered from flower to flower, softly humming to themselves. Tiny wrens called for food from their hidden nesting places. And sometimes when the wind roamed around the ancient house this hanging green haven would come alive with an eager rustling and to the old man dozing under the orange and yellow handkerchief in his deep armchair on the grass below the sound was as faint and soothing as the sea.

On that morning, though, the old man was nowhere to be seen. The cold winds of winter had almost finished their work of dismantling the leaves and flowers of the wall and the stones beneath showed through much more clearly. Just one slightly more sheltered place remained, under the overhanging eaves where the telephone wire joined the roof, a cosy little bower of leaves, with a few flowers embalmed by the icy blast, a place which was brittle and dusty and smelling of summer and here Wake and Bess took refuge. Perched on the wire running through the middle of this hiding place they scarcely dared to move because every time they did something would break away and go cascading down the wall, threatening to give them away. But they were out of sight and able to see everything happening in the garden.

Wake kept his eyes firmly fixed on the lady jackdaw. The night before he had found her extremely unfriendly as she stamped about the roof ridiculing his plan. This morning it was clear that she was in charge of it. He was familiar enough with the ways of jackdaws to know that they were behaving exactly as they would be expected to; every so often one or other of them would move to a different tree, or fly down to peck at the soil of the back garden. It was a moment or two before even he noticed something rather curious; every time the lady jackdaw changed her position she seemed to finish up just a little nearer to the house.

All morning the jackdaws maintained their watch on the house, observed by the two swallows under the eaves. Wake was surprised by his own patience. Never in his life before had he remained in the same position for so long whilst not actually sleeping. For her part, Bess solved the problem of remaining still by actually falling asleep. These days, hungry and cold for most of the time, they all seemed unusually sleepy.

He had actually started to think that the people in the farmhouse intended to remain indoors until the winter was over when at last things began to happen. Below them the kitchen door opened and a young woman appeared. She was holding an enormous basket. It was filled with clothes and she used both hands to hold it as she moved across the garden to a washing line strung between the branches of two trees. One by one the woman picked the clothes up from the basket and began to peg them up. Her hands were still red from the wash and from time to time she paused to cup them to her mouth, blowing on them so that her breath streamed out in the still, frosty air.

The pile of washing in the basket grew smaller. The line of washing grew longer and then at last the basket was empty. The woman stepped back a little to admire the effect of the brightly coloured garments sagging between the two trees and because they looked as cheerful as a line of flags she gave a little salute and grinned. Wake glanced swiftly along the faintly steaming clothes line. Most of the objects hanging there were people-shaped, in various colours and sizes, but of the orange handkerchief with the yellow sun in the centre there was no sign. Nor had he really expected that there would be. So what did the jackdaw intend to do? In a moment the woman would be retracing her steps to return inside the house and still she had made no move.

It was in that moment that the lady jackdaw performed an action so swift, so unexpected and so valiant that young swallows listening to the story of the Winter Crossing in the years to come would often gasp with fear and joy and sometimes even beg the teller of the story to go back a little bit and tell it all again.

As the two swallows watched transfixed from their hiding place under the eaves the woman stooped to pick up the heavy washing basket and as she did so her back was completely turned to the back door of the farmhouse. Wake realised in that moment that it was the first time this had happened and it was obviously the opportunity the lady jackdaw had been waiting for. She launched herself from her perch in the tree nearest to the house and alighted on the grass at the very edge of the gravel path running along the back of the building. From there she hopped swiftly on to the kitchen step. For a brief moment she paused there to glance back at her two companions sitting in the distant tree. In her eyes there was a sort of regret. And then she was gone, disappearing from sight inside the house.

Even though they were completely hidden from her sight Wake and Bess stiffened in apprehension as the woman began retracing her steps across the lawn towards them. They could hear the crunch of her slippers on the crisp grass of the frosty lawn and as she came nearer they took the only action which seemed appropriate; they closed their eyes. And then the woman had passed below them and entered the house. The door banged shut. Once more the garden was silent and deserted with everything exactly the same as it had been before. Except for the fact that somewhere in the strange and dangerous world lying beyond the farmhouse door there was now.... a jackdaw.

* * *

Chapter 8

Since we are now to accompany the lady jackdaw during the most hazardous exploit that she or any other of her kind had ever embarked upon I do feel it is important at this point to try to understand how it was that fate chose her and her alone to be the one who volunteered for the enterprise which was to enshrine the name of the jackdaws for ever in the illustrious and immortal legend of the Winter Crossing. The fact was that she could never resist a dare!

How many troubles are caused in this life by those three little words: "I dare you!" There can be something perfectly awful, something you would never dream of doing, until someone sidles up and murmurs this sinister challenge. It may involve going to the very edge, or up to the very top, or even down to the very bottom. You don't want to do it. You know it is unwise to do it. The person who suggested it would never dream of doing it. But who can resist those three awful words: "I dare you."

This had been the explanation for the jackdaw's mood of the night before. The anger she displayed to Wake was directed really at herself because the moment she heard why he had made the journey to the place where the jackdaws lived it was inevitable what would happen, particularly when you reflect that all the dares she had ever accepted had been concerned with the opportunity of stealing, or to put it a little more legally, acquiring something for her collection.

Over the years she had taken some quite appalling risks, all because some foolish jackdaw who did not have her best interests at heart had said: "Go on, I dare you." She had acquired things from tables set out in the garden, as people actually dozed in chairs nearby. She had hopped up on to window ledges and leaned inside to acquire things. And on one terrifying occasion she had actually hopped through an open bathroom window and along the tiled ledge inside to acquire a glittering ring left there by a lady in the understandable belief that it was safe. Never in her reckless career, though, had she ever contemplated entering the home of Man, in the certain knowledge that the door would close shut behind her trapping her inside.

Now, inside the farmhouse kitchen, alert and frightened, straining to interpret the meaning of the faint noises and distant movements of the house, the lady jackdaw was honest enough to keep reminding herself that it was all her own appalling fault.

It had been her intention to seek out the first hiding place she could find and take refuge there until nightfall and this was clearly not to be found in the kitchen. She knew this the moment she hopped through the back door. The room was bathed in a bright cheery light and there were disturbing indications of human occupation; a fire glowed cheerily behind the glass-fronted stove and on top of it a pan was gently simmering.

The jackdaw also saw something else, something she had not been expecting and the sight of it set her heart pounding wildly at the knowledge of just how close she had come to disaster. From her vantage point outside she had often watched the young woman working in the kitchen and had always assumed that she was in there alone. Now she realised her mistake. Below the level of the window and undetectable from outside there were several chairs. A low armchair was pulled up close to the glowing stove; the others were arranged along two sides of a long wooden table. All the chairs were empty but it was only by chance that she had avoided hopping straight into a room full of people! Close to panic the jackdaw fled out of the kitchen by the far door and as she went she heard the loud slam of the outer door finally closing on her only route to freedom.

Beyond the kitchen lay a long hallway. The floor was made of wood, dark and uneven, covered in rough matting stretching all the way to the door at the front of the house. After her panic in the kitchen the jackdaw was relieved to see that it was quite deserted. Halfway down the hall a large piece of furniture stood against the wall. There was a large mirror in the centre of it and the hooks on either side were draped with all kinds of human garments, some of them reaching right down to the floor. It was the perfect hiding place.

Swiftly she darted across the hall and squeezed herself into the narrow gap between the coat-stand and the wall. There, satisfied that she could not be seen, even by someone standing directly in front of her, the jackdaw froze into immobility and settled down to wait for the freedom of the night when she would carry out her task.

Outside, in the gloom of a wintry afternoon, the old farmhouse was submitting comfortably to the fury of yet another of the countless storms it had weathered over the centuries. The wind was sweeping in across the estuary from the west in waves like the sea. Great gusts shook the house and the rain pattered like spray against the windows. From all over the house came the steady sound of running water as the rain dripped from the eaves of the roof and ran gurgling along the gutters and down the drainpipes. Listening to all these distant sounds from her place of concealment in the hall the jackdaw was aware of the enormous presence of the house enclosing her. Two doors--the one leading back from the hall into the kitchen and the one leading out into the back garden--now lay between her and freedom. Out there the power of instant flight had protected her from danger; inside this place those glossy black wings lay folded and useless at her sides. If danger threatened nothing could save her, for there was no escape. By now her companions would have left the garden to seek shelter from the storm. She was completely alone. And she had only a vague idea about what to do next.

One unexpected problem had already arisen. She had noticed it moments earlier as she fled out from the kitchen and into the hall. Almost opposite the kitchen door lay the room where the old man would sit in winter to gaze out across the garden. Her original idea had been to enter it cautiously at a moment of her choosing but the door was closed and there was no way of telling when it would open again. When it did open there would be no time to worry about what lay on the other side. She would have to enter and take her chances.

She was still thinking about those unknown dangers when the door of that room opened. She heard the old man's voice murmuring from inside the room and then an enormous black cat strolled casually out into the hall and began stretching itself just a few feet away from her hiding place. Outside the house the storm still raged but in the shadowy hallway there was only a deep and dreadful silence in which the jackdaw struggled to control her panic. Every instinct was urging her to flee, to open her wings and rise upwards away from this danger and yet she knew her wings were useless. Her only chance lay in concealment.

The cat paused between the two doors, her tail swinging idly from side to side, apparently undecided about what to do next, gazing casually down the hall towards the coat-stand. Staring back from the shadows the jackdaw was convinced their eyes had met and that at any moment the cat would come padding down the hallway to investigate. But she seemed unsuspicious. Lazily she rolled over on the matting and began to groom herself, anointing her long, gleaming flanks with a startlingly pink tongue. From time to time she would stop suddenly and gaze intently down the hall as though she had heard something. Softly the jackdaw closed her eyes to shut out the sight.

She was only persuaded to open them again by a new sound in the hall; the sound of scratching, as the cat scraped at the closed kitchen door with those fearful claws. As the sound went unheeded she began to meow until at last the door was opened from inside. Light flooded into the hall. A woman's voice gently reproached her and then the door closed again and the shadows were restored. Almost as though it was not really a part of her the jackdaw listened to her own heartbeat as it slowly returned to normal.

It was now apparent that the house was coming to life again after the languor of the gloomy winter afternoon. She could hear human sounds coming from behind the kitchen door; they were the voices of children. As the excited sounds of their homecoming grew louder the door of the other room opened. A tall, slightly stooping figure emerged and slowly crossed the hall to enter the kitchen. It was the old man from the garden and he had left the door open.

This was her chance. The jackdaw darted from her hiding place and along the hall to the door and began to push against it with her folded wing. It would not move. Just behind the opposite door, even closer now, she could hear the excited chatter of the children in the kitchen. She pictured the door bursting open, flooding the hall with light, filling it with people. She braced herself more firmly on the matting beneath her feet and pushed again. This time the door yielded to the pressure of her body; it was only a few inches but it was enough. She slipped into the room.

It was now growing dark but the lights in the room had not yet been switched on. The curtains were open and the windows still ran with rain; beyond the glass her own familiar world had dissolved into a deep and featureless grey. Never to her knowledge in the long history of the jackdaws had one of them ever watched the night descend from inside one of the homes of Man. She felt utterly alone.

In the hearth the embers of what had been a steeply-banked fire glowed red and still. In this faint light the jackdaw could distinguish only the main features of the room but it was already familiar to her from her observations through the window. She knew that two deep, old armchairs stood on either side of the hearth and that the one farthest from the window was the one in which the old man liked to sit. The chair had a floral cover reaching all the way down to the floor and this was the hiding place she had chosen. Hopping swiftly across the shadowy room the jackdaw used her beak to lift the bottom edge of the cover behind the chair and slipped under its folds, allowing it to fall down behind her like a curtain.

Faintly from across the hallway she could still hear the sounds of the family but the silence surrounding her was like the silence of an empty room. It seemed almost impossible that she could be sharing that silence with another living creature and yet she knew that she was not alone. She listened intently. Had the little yellow bird seen her enter the room?

Ever since the jackdaws had first devised their plan it had been the little yellow bird which had caused her most concern. Neither she nor any of the other jackdaws had been able to understand the reason for confining it in a cage. They found it hard to believe that it might be dangerous and had finally come to the painful conclusion that it was being punished in some way. Whatever the explanation the captive bird was clearly different from all other birds because it lived with Man. And because it was different it was impossible to predict what it might do; as the little yellow bird now amply demonstrated.

"I do hope you'll make yourself comfortable," said the voice. "We don't often see a jackdaw in here."

The jackdaw said nothing in the remote hope that there might just be another jackdaw in the room.

"I'm sorry I'm not able to greet you personally," the voice continued, "but may I suggest that you remain where you are for the time being?"

Carefully the jackdaw lifted the cover at the back of the chair and put her head out, just far enough to be able to stare across at the shadows in the window.

"Pardon?"

"The old man will be returning at any moment from the kitchen and when he does he will put the lights on and have his afternoon tea. It might be better if you were not actually standing in the middle of the room when that happened."

Never in her life before had the jackdaw been addressed with such old-world courtesy. Out in the wild such niceties tended to be neglected and she was somewhat at a loss as to how she should respond. In vain she tried to think of something equally gracious to say in return. It was clear, however, that the little yellow bird's conversational powers were more than equal to the social problem of awkward little pauses.

"It is a thoroughly nasty afternoon. You must be quite relieved to be indoors."

The little yellow bird gave no indication that he was interested in knowing why she was there.

"You're right," agreed the jackdaw. "I came in to see if I could get dry."

"Quite so," said the little yellow bird gravely.

Despite the gracious elegance of the conversation the jackdaw was still alert and highly suspicious. It was far and away the oddest way of speaking she had ever encountered and clearly acquired as a result of living among humans. And that raised the important question of whose side this curious little bird was really on. In short, was he to be trusted? If he was indeed her enemy in his own environment he would probably prove to be a formidable one.

For his part the little yellow bird seemed untroubled by these weighty matters and continued to treat her with the sort of attentive courtesy which is quite likely to turn the head of a jackdaw reared in the wild, with all the social limitations this implies.

"You're probably quite worried about the cat," continued the disembodied voice, "but please don't trouble yourself. She is very old and it's a long time since she's even been aware that I'm in the room and if she does become suspicious I can always create a diversion."

The jackdaw who had so far been unable to think of anything to say now recovered a little of her poise.

"Oh, please don't create anything on my account," she said politely. "I'll be gone by the morning."

"No explanations for the moment," said the voice suavely. "We'll have a little chat later and then you can tell me exactly why you're here."

Motionless in her hiding place behind the chair, the jackdaw now listened in fascination to the strange and unfamiliar sounds of a human family settling down for the evening in their own habitat.[10]

She could not of course actually see anything from her hiding place behind the chair and all her impressions were based on what she could hear. She heard the man return to the room and put the lights on.

She listened as he tended the fire and then she felt the chair pressed hard against her back as he sat down with a deep, contented sigh. Into the room soon afterwards came a young woman she assumed to be the one she had watched in the garden and a little while later they were joined by another man; he, she decided, must be the one she would see working in the fields. Finally two children, possibly three, entered the room from the kitchen and with the family now all together again the jackdaw heard the awful sound of yet another door closing between her and the world outside. In truth, though, she was far too fascinated by the things she was hearing to be really afraid.

There was the murmur of voices and occasional laughter. Once she heard a loud burst of sound, reminiscent of music, followed by a roar of protest from the chair and instant silence.

More voices murmured for a while and then she heard a new sound; something very small was being rattled furiously in a container of some kind and then flung across a flat surface to the accompaniment of loud squeals of excitement and protest. On occasion throughout the evening there was the gurgle and splash of things being poured. Once this was followed by loud choking sounds and an urgent thumping which shook the armchair above her. Most puzzling of all, towards the end of the evening, was a deep and regular wheezing sound involving one and possibly two humans. It started very quietly and gradually grew to an absolute crescendo; since the children greeted this noise with appreciative though muffled laughter the jackdaw decided it must be some kind of human entertainment.

Watching the room from outside in the darkness the jackdaws had been able to establish that evenings in the farmhouse always

---

[10] *So far as we know she was the first jackdaw ever to observe the behaviour of humans in this way and it is worth noting in passing that she received (and accepted) many invitations to speak about her experiences in later years.*

ended in the same way. One by one, starting with the youngest, the family would retire upstairs for the night. To her relief, for she had not moved and scarcely breathed for several hours, the jackdaw became aware at last that this was happening. One by one the members of the family said their farewells and left the room for the night until there was silence and it was clear that only the old man still remained, a heavy presence in the chair above her. Eventually she felt the heavy weight of the armchair lift as he, too, rose to his feet. There was a vigorous raking sound from the hearth and then the old man was walking across the room. The light went out and the door softly closed behind him.

Carefully the jackdaw raised the hem of the chair cover and peered out. The fire had now revived and shadows leapt and fell soundlessly all around the room. In the dim light she could just discern the golden cage hanging in the window. It was still and silent and she wondered if the little yellow bird was now asleep. Still without moving she continued to study her surroundings, noting that above her an ancient crystal chandelier hung down from the ceiling; in an emergency that might just prove useful. Scarcely breathing she concentrated on listening for any other sound in the room. The voice which now addressed her was studiously loud and calm, as though impatient with her caution.

"There is really no cause for anxiety," said the little yellow bird. "We are alone. She always sleeps in the kitchen. The cat, I mean. Perhaps you would now like to come over to the window where I can see you?"

The jackdaw was disconcerted to find that even perched on the windowsill she could not see the little yellow bird clearly. The firelight scarcely reached the alcove in the window where the cage hung down and all she could discern were the little bird's eyes and something about them worried her. It might have been her imagination but it seemed as though they glittered with a strange and feverish excitement.

"Welcome," said the voice from the shadows. "I do hope your wait was not too uncomfortable. And now do please tell me what brings you here tonight and if I can be of any assistance."

The jackdaw mumbled something about coming into the house "for a look-round", forgetting the time and finding herself trapped when all the doors closed for the night. She quite forgot that she had already told the little yellow bird that she had entered the house to escape the storm but if he remembered he made no comment.

"I'm just waiting until morning and then I'll be off."

"Anything in particular?"

The jackdaw struggled for composure. "Pardon?"

"Were you 'looking round' for anything in particular or were you merely browsing? I know you are something of a collector."

Once more the jackdaw found herself at something of a disadvantage. She had entered the farmhouse convinced of her own ability to cope with the problem of the little yellow bird. Any creature living in the wild was bound to be superior to one which spent its days confined in a cage. What she had not expected was that she would feel so awkward in the presence of this suave little stranger. His gracious manner seemed to suggest that he regarded her arrival in the house as some sort of social occasion and she could not help feeling slightly self-conscious about the fact that she was actually there to steal something. On a rather more personal level she was also anxious about her appearance. Since the onset of winter the bad weather had played havoc with her feathers and in the presence of this exceedingly smooth and sophisticated bird she was very much aware of not exactly looking her best.

But the charm and openness of his manner had also had another unexpected effect. She felt a growing inclination to trust this strange little bird, to reveal the reason for her presence in the house and even to ask for his help. But how could she be sure that his loyalties were not now to this human family who fed and cared for him, rather than to the birds of the forest with whom he had so little in common? Before matters progressed any further she would have to find out.

"I still can't understand why you are locked up in a cage," she said solicitously. "Have you committed some crime? Or are you perhaps dangerous?"

The little yellow bird laughed. "They keep me here to sing for them."

"To sing for them?"

"They feed me. They keep me warm. They are really very kind and all I am required to do is sing. It's not a bad life. Not that I always feel like singing, though."

"What kind of a bird are you?" the jackdaw inquired.

"I'm not exactly sure of the proper scientific name." The little yellow bird seemed slightly embarrassed by this admission and

71

quickly added: "One thing I do know, however, is that I am not the only one."

"You mean there are other little yellow birds in other cages?"

"I mean there are others which are free. Birds which fly. We do have wings you know." At this the jackdaw was astonished to hear a fluttering sound from the darkness of the cage, followed by a metallic chime as the little yellow bird attempted to fly upwards and almost instantaneously hit the roof of the cage.

"There," said the little yellow bird. "There is somewhere where birds like me fly around like that all day, a place where there are no cages. I am not aware exactly where it is but what I do know is that it is far away from here, in a place where it never rains and the wind is never too cold. A place where being yellow doesn't mean that all the other birds consider you to be different and strange."

From the darkness of the cage came the playful tinkle of a tiny bell as the captive hurried along his perch and pressed his head urgently against the bars.

"Don't forget where this cage hangs. From here in the window almost every day I sit and watch you all out there. Every so often I choose a bird and then I pretend that I am out there flying alongside him. I may even have flown in this way with you. So you see, I am a bird just like you." And at these words he beat one of his wings savagely against the bars of the cage. "Or almost like you." All at once he seemed overcome by embarrassment. "Do please forgive me. I am not usually so emotional."

Outside the storm had ceased. The family upstairs seemed to have settled down for the night. They were now conversing in hushed whispers, like old friends. Casually the jackdaw murmured: "I know a little bird who by now should have gone back to a place very like the one you describe. But he cannot leave."

"I know about these birds which live in two places," came the voice through the darkness. "I have watched them go and I have watched them return. Why is it not possible for your friend to leave?"

This was the moment when the jackdaw took the decision to behave in a way so out of character that the thought of what she had done would trouble her for several hours afterwards. Never in her life before had she been so appallingly truthful. She had always conducted her affairs, especially those concerned with collecting things, on the basic principle that no one was to be trusted.

Conversation was designed to give as little as possible away; concealing, denying, pretending; these were the conversational skills she had perfected. But now she completely abandoned these high principles in what seemed to her in retrospect to have been a disturbing lapse from her usual impeccable standards. Even so the jackdaw could not bring herself to be totally frank. She explained how Creakwing had been unable to travel south with the other swallows and how a group of younger birds had remained behind to assist him in a desperate attempt to complete the journey before the winter became too severe but she did not mention the precise nature of her mission. At the end of her account she said simply: "I am here tonight to try to help Creakwing."

"Let me help." There was something like desperation in the captive's voice. "If your plan has brought you here I can surely help."

With an inward shudder the jackdaw revealed another secret. "There is something here which I need; something which is vital to the plan."

She began to explain that she had entered the house to take possession of a handkerchief... a very special handkerchief with a round yellow sun at the centre and yellow beams radiating outwards from it across a wide orange sky. She did not say why she required it and the little yellow bird seemed too excited by this description to inquire.

"It's here," he cried triumphantly. "It's here in this room." In his eagerness to help he appeared for a moment to be trying to force his way out between the bars of the cage. "It's over there. In the old man's chair. Under the cushion. He uses it to cover his face when he's having a little sleep. Go and see."

"Thank you," said the jackdaw calmly. "That is a great relief, I must say. But I still have to get it out of the house, you know. And for that I must wait until morning."

"Tell me about the plan," pleaded the prisoner. "Tell me while we wait."

In all the excitement of preparing to enter the farmhouse and steal the handkerchief the jackdaw had scarcely given a thought to the purpose of her mission. She had also overlooked her own reservations about Wake's plan. Describing it now for the very first time she could not help feeling that it sounded both reckless and doomed. This, however, was not the reaction of the little yellow bird.

"All the way to Africa," he murmured reverently. "I've never heard of anything so brave. Don't you see? Africa must be where they live, the others like me. Even if they do not live in Africa it must be somewhere very like it. If only for that reason you must permit me to help."

Still clinging to the residual remnants of her former sly discretion the jackdaw decided that first she would establish that the little yellow bird was at least telling the truth about the handkerchief, so she hopped down from the windowsill and over to the old man's chair. She rummaged with her beak underneath the cushion. Sure enough it was there. With her beak gripping a corner of the handkerchief she pulled it out and draped it across the arm of the chair. By the fitful light of the dying fire she studied it. So this was the key to the whole enterprise? Using this nondescript and flimsy scrap of silk the swallows intended to try to escape from the encroaching winter to their home in the south. As she gazed down at the handkerchief, the little yellow bird interrupted her rather sombre thoughts by gently shaking the bars of his cage to remind her of his presence. She returned to the windowsill.

"I dare say he will be very puzzled when he finds that it has gone," said the little yellow bird.

Since a close examination had only confirmed her belief that she had no wish to add the handkerchief to her private collection the jackdaw murmured nobly that when it was all over they must try to ensure that it was returned.

The bars of the cage rang with excitement once again. "Now you have it you must tell me how I can help."

The three jackdaws involved in the enterprise had spent most of the previous night devising their plan for seizing the handkerchief. It was a plan which depended on the most meticulous timing and co-ordination, both by her and by the other two outside, if it was to have any prospect of success. There would be only one chance. If they failed she might very well die and so in all probability would the swallows. And yet here she was actually contemplating a change in that plan to accommodate the enthusiasm of this strange little bird.

On the other hand, how could she refuse his offer of help? The jackdaw was not often moved by sentimental considerations; thieves who allowed their finer feelings to prevail rather let the side down but due to what she perceived as an unsuspected weakness of character in herself she had allowed herself to be deeply moved by the plight of this sad little prisoner. It was quite clear that behind all that odd dignity and courtesy there lay a great loneliness. For all his brave words he was not part of her world but her unexpected appearance in the room where he was imprisoned had clearly convinced him that for the first time in his life he might become briefly involved with it; not only involved but assisting. How could she reject him? Particularly when she was beginning to perceive a way in which he *could* help. The role she was thinking of was perfectly suited to his situation and if it succeeded it would have the added advantage of speeding things up considerably.

As she began to explain she could hear the little yellow bird shuffling about restlessly on his perch, unable to control his excitement, but when she finished speaking all his old courtliness had returned, enhanced now by the new and stirring sensation of being involved at last in such momentous concerns.

"It must succeed. It will succeed, "he said and his voice rang with a high and noble resolution.

"We'll know in the morning," responded the jackdaw soberly.

* * *

Chapter 9

The first faint light of dawn summoned them to action, like the distant call of a trumpet.

In his cage in the window the little yellow bird gave every indication that he had remained in a state of excitement all through the night. As the garden began to appear again in the misty morning light his eyes scanned it eagerly and the cage swayed on the end of its chain as he rushed from one end of the perch to the other, trying to enhance his view. Perched on the arm of the old man's chair the jackdaw observed his movements with growing apprehension. Upstairs a lone voice was singing, a prelude, she assumed, to the awakening dawn chorus of a human family. It was a sound which served to remind her that the little yellow bird was a great deal closer to these humans than to the wild birds of the forest. The jackdaw was beginning to feel the very special kind of unease experienced only by the conspirator who has perhaps revealed too much. Was it possible that she had made a profound mistake in altering the plan at the last-minute simply because this odd little bird had pleaded so fervently to be allowed to help?

What she had not fully appreciated was the confusion the change of plan might cause. Her two companions outside the house knew nothing about her new ally. They would probably disapprove. But more importantly, if they did not react instantly to the changed situation it would be disastrous. One chance, that was all they had. And they might lose it because of her sentimental gesture towards a bird in a cage who probably felt a great deal more affection for his human benefactors than he felt for her. She was still gloomily pondering on the most tactful way of informing the little yellow bird that his services would not be required when there was a cry of excitement from the window.

"The jackdaws are here!"

The jackdaw hurried across to the window and gazed out. Once more her heart had started beating wildly but out there all was still and quiet. The spell of the night still lay upon the garden. Nothing moved. Not even the two jackdaws who had silently appeared from out of the mist and were now sitting in a tree directly in front of the window. The jackdaw was troubled to note the glittering object gripped in her husband's beak, a reminder of how carefully they had formulated the details of the plan they were about to carry out.

The sounds of movement and voices could now be heard all over the house. Feet trod heavily on the floor above. That first lone voice of the human dawn chorus had now been swelled by loud musical instruments. The jackdaw glanced out at her two companions watching impassively from the tree. Were they, too, aware that the house was coming awake? As though responding to the thought both birds rose from their perch and swooped down on to the outside ledge of the window. Separated from her now by only a thin sheet of glass her husband grinned at her so enormously that the ring threatened to fall from his beak. And then the broad grin turned to a frown as he became aware for the first time of the eager little bird watching him from the cage which hung beside her. But there was no way for her to explain, nor was there time; she could hear footsteps in the hall.

Turning away from the window she returned to the old man's chair, lunged for the handkerchief with her beak and without pausing fluttered up to the chandelier. The effect was unexpected. As she alighted on the rim the chandelier began swaying wildly, so that she had to cling on desperately with her head more or less jammed among the tinkling crystal pieces, realising at the same time that a substantial corner of the handkerchief was hanging down below her.

The glass was still faintly chiming when the door opened and the woman entered the room. Clinging precariously to the rim of the chandelier the jackdaw froze and her dark shape merged with the shadows around the ceiling. Only in that moment did it occur to her that the women might now press the switch which would light up her hiding place! But the room was just light enough. The women ignored the switch and walked across the room towards the fireplace. She did not look up. She was holding a poker above the ashes of the fire and yawning contentedly when the disturbance began.

From his cage in the window the little yellow bird shrieked wildly. The woman rose from her crouching position in front of the fireplace and stared in amazement towards the cage.

"What on earth?...."[11]

---

[11] *These words and those which follow were not actually remembered by the jackdaw, since her species does not understand human speech. I have been able to reconstruct what was said by calling personally at the farm in*

From her splendid vantage point just under the ceiling the jackdaw was so fascinated to observe the plan actually unfolding before her eyes that she forgot to be frightened. Outside, her husband was standing boldly on the windowsill in the strengthening morning light, with his companion beside him. His beak was pointed upwards. In it was a blood-red ring, glowing richly as he turned it in the air. Because he was so close she could see something unexpected in his face. He kept glancing anxiously into the room at the cage in which the little yellow bird was panicking so dramatically. The original idea had been for the jackdaws to stand on the windowsill flaunting the ruby ring until someone in the house eventually noticed them. This uncertainty had been removed with the intervention of the little yellow bird but the birds outside were of course unaware of the change of plan; they assumed that the prisoner was trying to ingratiate himself with his captors by betraying the jackdaws. That, she realised, was the explanation for those desperate and accusing glances.

If this reaction had upset the little yellow bird he gave no sign of it for now he redoubled his efforts. Once more he let out that cry of alarm and then for good measure he jumped up and down on his perch, so that the cage shook wildly and the bars rang like the strings of a harp. The woman who had been staring blankly at the commotion in the cage rose to her feet. "What on earth's got into you this morning?" she demanded and strode swiftly across the room to the window. Standing beside the cage she glared down at the occupant, followed his agitated gaze out into the garden. And screamed.

"My ruby ring! The jackdaws had it all the time."

It was the reaction they had been waiting for. As the scream rang out the jackdaws swung their heads around and glared into the house. The woman banged furiously on the glass.

"You leave it alone. That's my ring. You just bring it back."

The jackdaw with the ring appeared to panic. His beak gaped open and the ring dropped out, down below the window out of sight

---

the guise of an interested visitor to the area who had heard about the strange affair of the ruby ring. The words were recalled for me by the lady who had actually used them. I am sorry for the deceit, especially the false beard, since the lady concerned made me a nice cup of tea with ginger sponge cake which is my favourite.

of the woman. Both birds hurriedly hopped down and disappeared from sight under the windowsill, clearly intent on recovering it. The woman seemed transfixed, uncertain what to do; whether to keep the jackdaws in sight until someone else arrived or dash outside to confront them. At that moment a boy appeared in the doorway, obviously attracted by her cries.

"The jackdaws have come back with my ring. Bold as brass." She was already hurrying towards the door. "They've just dropped it under the window. Keep an eye on them while I go and fetch it."

Everything depended on what the woman did next. If she behaved as they had predicted all would be well; if not she was trapped and doomed. High up in the chandelier the jackdaw watched her rush from the room and out into the hall. So far so good; she had left the door open. But the boy still remained in the room. Once more the woman cried out, this time from outside the house. Her cry was too much for the little boy. Unable to control his excitement he, too, deserted his post under the window and rushed out of the room.

In a confusion of glittering light and tinkling glass the jackdaw disentangled herself from the chandelier and dropped to the floor. The open door beckoned. Beyond it she could sense the whole world, more precious to her now than ever after her night in the house. Out in the hall she saw with relief that the door leading into the kitchen was also open. In their desperation to recover the ruby ring the family were behaving exactly as the jackdaws had predicted. With the precious handkerchief trailing from her beak she hopped swiftly across the deserted hall and into the kitchen. Was it really only yesterday that she had made this journey from the other direction? The outer door was also open to the morning. Moving towards it she scanned the kitchen anxiously. There was no sign of the cat. She was almost at the door and her features were actually lighting up with the triumph of that splendid moment when disaster struck.

Far away at the front of the house someone opened the door. A fierce draught swept through the kitchen. Desperately the jackdaw flung herself back and just escaped being crushed as the outer door of the kitchen slammed shut in front of her. The movement was so decisive that it almost seemed as though her presence had been discovered at the very last moment. Instinctively the jackdaw once more sought refuge, this time in a narrow space between the stove and the sink.

Next moment she knew why someone had opened the front door so disastrously, as the cat strolled into the kitchen. For a moment she paused, sniffing the air and gazing around the room with amiable menace and then she padded noiselessly across the floor and lowered her dark head to a feeding bowl under the table. The jackdaw pressed herself back against the wall. But because the woman and the boy were still outside the house her ordeal this time was not to be prolonged. There was a rattle from the door handle. The door opened and the woman returned to the kitchen, calling out excitedly. This time the door to freedom stayed open.

In her hiding place, poised for flight, the jackdaw took a deep breath. She could not actually see into the room. Was the cat still quietly feeding, or was he watching? Silently she screamed a command to her own faltering spirits. And then, in an awkward, fluttering motion, not quite flying and not quite running, she sped across the kitchen, past the little boy who was just entering from the garden and a moment later, in a soaring, cawing outburst of relief and triumph, she was climbing into the morning mist above the farmhouse, trailing the bright colours of her trophy across the sky behind her like a banner.

From his prison in the window the little yellow bird watched her go. Steadfastly, his gaze followed her long upward flight and even when she disappeared from sight behind the corner of the building he scampered along his perch to keep her in view. At last, even with his head pressed hard against the bars he could see her no longer. The sky was empty.

He turned from the window to discover the whole family had now gathered in the room and were marvelling over the events they had just witnessed. The ruby ring had clearly been in the possession of the jackdaws for some considerable time and the part that he had played in its return had astonished them all.

The woman stood in the centre of the room, twirling her hand in the air to reflect the light from the ring and admiring it all over again.

"I would never have noticed the jackdaws playing with it if it hadn't been for him."

A face loomed beside the cage and a man said: "Who's a clever boy, then?" and then the little boy appeared and mimicked the words. And when no one was looking an even younger child paid her tribute by shaking his cage affectionately from side to side and the little yellow bird, who was used to it, flexed his tiny feet around the wooden perch and waited for his home to stop swinging. For once he was not enjoying all this human attention, as he struggled with what was for him a very unusual sensation, the feeling that he was not really part of the life of this human family at all. He was also feeling just a little bit sorry for himself and as we all know that is just about as sorrowful as it is possible to be. He was feeling sorry for himself because of the rather perfunctory way in which he and the jackdaw had parted. He had rather hoped that before leaving his new friend would say something momentous about the experience they had just shared, with perhaps a passing reference to the assistance he had rendered. Instead the jackdaw had fled from the room without a word or a backward glance leaving him to endure these human attentions, all the more tiresome because they were based on a quite erroneous interpretation of his part in the affair.

It had been the most fascinating night of his life. Once the jackdaw had revealed her plan and the part he was to play in it they passed the time until morning by talking. As a prisoner confined in a cage he naturally enough had very little to talk about and so instead he listened spellbound to the jackdaw's tales about the great world outside. Since his knowledge of the world ended with the old brick wall at the bottom of the garden he was obliged to accept that everything the jackdaw said was true but it was amazing all the same.

He had been especially stirred by the incredible exploit of the swallows. Ever since he was old enough to notice such things he had observed that every winter they disappeared. One day he would be watching them admiringly from his cage, as they fed spectacularly in the skies above the farmhouse and next day they would be gone. At first he had vaguely assumed that they spent the winter sheltering in some way from the cold and the damp.[12]

---

[12] *This is not as silly as it seems. For a long time it was believed that swallows hibernated during the winter UNDER WATER! How they were supposed to do this was never satisfactorily explained since no one was prepared to spend the winter under water finding out.*

Now he had learned the truth about their incredible journey he found himself gazing up into the sky in the direction he knew instinctively led to that southern land where the swallows spent the winter. The mystery of migration fascinated him because he had the odd feeling that he actually knew the land the swallows went to. He knew this could not possibly be true because he had lived in a cage for as long as he could remember. And yet whenever he found himself thinking about the place where the swallows went his sadness certainly felt true.[13]

He knew there was no possibility that he would ever return to the south, (for he always thought of it as "going back"), but he had been able to take some pleasure from the knowledge that he had perhaps been of assistance in ensuring that the swallows made the journey. Sitting alone in his cage, however, he was now beginning to think that his involvement in the events of that morning had not perhaps been so very important after all; the jackdaws could probably have carried out their plan without him. But he did wish the lady jackdaw had not left him so abruptly and that the two birds outside had not glared at him with quite such fierce contempt, as though they were convinced that he was trying to betray them.

I have to tell you now that what happened next was vouched for by a little girl and so it must be true and the only reason you have never heard of it before is because I am the only one who knows anything about it, as I will explain.

One of the problems of childhood to which far too little attention has been paid concerns the plight of those children who observe something extremely interesting in their early years but are unable to speak of it until they have learned to talk which sometimes takes so long that by the time they have learned the words to describe it they have usually forgotten all about it. Who knows what they might say if only they could speak? It is a sombre thought.

---

[13] *Sorry about providing another footnote so soon after the previous one but it is rather interesting and should be read if you have the time. I just thought I should point that the little yellow bird was only partly correct. His species does originate in the south but not precisely where the swallows come from; they are from a group of islands called the Azores where they are green, not yellow and, of course, totally free. How the little captive was aware of all this it is not for me to say.*

The reason I mention this problem is because the only human witness of the happening I am about to describe was a minute little girl (the one whose hobby was shaking the cage from side to side). She could not describe what she had seen until she had learned to talk and by then she had seen so many other wonderful things that it had quite slipped her mind. The truth finally emerged a long time later, at the end of a day when the sight of a group of jackdaws had jogged her memory. In the close and trusting atmosphere of bedtime, she whispered the story to her mother, before a goodnight kiss, and during the aforementioned visit, in disguise, to the farm I learned about it, too.

This is her account of what happened. Everyone but the little girl had left the room after all the excitement involving the return of the ring. She had woken up one of her dolls and was engaged in dressing it. The captive yellow bird was gazing idly down at her from his perch in the cage when she just happened to glance out through the window.

Out there in the garden, just where the mist began, so vague and dreamy that it was perfectly possible to believe they were not really there at all, a number of birds had silently appeared. There were nine of them, arranged in a little semi-circle on the frosty grass and looking up at the window; three jackdaws in the middle, with three swallows on either side. The jackdaw in the centre of this silent arc of watchers was draped from head to toe in the folds of a yellow and orange handkerchief, so long that it trailed behind her like a cloak on the grass. Something glittered at her throat, so that the moment seemed even more serious and ceremonial.

The birds were dangerously close to the place where the humans lived but their eyes were calm and unafraid. Slowly, as the only tiny, human witness gazed out in wonder, the jackdaw in the cloak of yellow and orange stepped to the front and in one single movement the visitors all bowed down their heads together towards the little yellow bird sitting in his cage in the window. Next moment they had stepped back into the mist, disappearing as silently as they had come, and the little girl was standing there alone in the window beside the cage, trying to decide for a long time afterwards if it really had happened and wishing with all her heart that she knew the words to describe what she had seen.

* * *

Chapter 10

There is a little game some people play when they find themselves separated by an enormous distance from someone they really care about. What they do is to sit down quietly somewhere and think very hard about the absent one, saying to themselves: "I wonder what so-and-so is doing AT THIS VERY MOMENT." It is not unknown, I am happy to re-assure you, for even quite small and insubstantial children to give rise to these thoughts. Well, we writers often do the same thing, only with one important difference. We have the technology which makes it possible for us to *know* what is happening hundreds or even thousands of miles away, without actually being there. And that is how I am able to tell you what was happening in the winter home of the swallows far away in Africa on the very morning that the jackdaws successfully carried out their part in the great plan

You may find it hard to believe that the swallows could have settled down so completely in their new home, within a few days of arriving there, but what you must remember is that there was to them nothing unfamiliar about Africa. Like all migrant birds they had two homes (rather in the way that some rich people have a home in the town and another in the country) and they just happened to have gone to stay in the other one, although for the birds which had never migrated before, of course, everything was new and unfamiliar and they did take some time to adjust to the new life. What made them all feel more at home was the fact that they were in a place very like the one they had left, except that the sun now shone every day, instead of intermittently and food was plentiful again.

Not all the birds which had set out on the long and dangerous journey had reached Africa. Among those which were missing were many newly-fledged swallows which had been travelling south for the first time. In the days after the arrival of the main group one or two stragglers did fly in and the moment they appeared in the northern sky all the others swarmed up to meet them with glad cries of joy. But as the days passed and the sky remained empty everyone assumed that the missing birds would not now be coming and life went on; except for those who remembered the missing swallows.

In the hottest part of the day, when the whole landscape seemed to pant and tremble in the heat, as all the other swallows roosted in the shade, one or two of their number still kept watch. They would find a vantage point which afforded an uninterrupted view of the whole northern sky and there they would sit patiently for hours on end gazing upwards and remembering little things about the missing birds.

Among those who still maintained this vigil were the four mothers of Wake and his companions. There was no one to watch for Creakwing. The swallows still talked of him with respect and affection but there were no relatives to keep vigil for him. It was also now widely accepted that he had never actually set out on the migration; the older swallows were all familiar with the true meaning of the ritual words about "following on later". Curiously enough none of the mothers ever discussed the possibility that there might be some connection between the old leader and their own missing offspring. They assumed that the six young swallows had set out with the main party and gone astray somewhere along the route to the south although it had been puzzling to discover that no one apparently remembered seeing any of them during the journey.

On that particular morning Wake's mother had been helping to pass the time by recalling his disapproval of the dawn chorus.

"He was so funny. He couldn't see the point of it; kept saying it woke people up and ought to be stopped. The dawn chorus-- stopped!"

The other three mothers looked at her sharply. "No doubt he'll still feel the same way when it wakes him up down here," said one of them firmly.

"If anything the sun comes up even earlier in Africa," said another.

Wake's mother knew that she was being gently chided for speaking of her son as though she was never going to see him again. They were reminding her that it was her duty to go on hoping.

"Of course," she murmured. "He won't be any different here."

But I wonder if the mothers keeping that long vigil on the warm plains of Africa would have been quite so steadfast if they had suspected that thousands of miles away to the north Wake and the others had still not even begun their Crossing...

On the morning that the daring mission to seize the handkerchief was successfully completed the six swallows gathered in the clearing where the jackdaws lived to consider their next move.

After obtaining the handkerchief it had seemed advisable to get as far away from the farm as possible and as a tribute to her exploit inside the farmhouse Wake had invited the heroine of the hour to become the temporary custodian of that precious object. The lady jackdaw had accepted the honour with no indication of reluctance and now, perched above him in the tree which grew up through the ruined floor of the cottage, surrounded by an admiring circle of friends and relations, she was reliving her exploit with admirable attention to detail.

As he listened to her account of events inside the farmhouse Wake was well aware that they were wasting valuable time but he was reluctant to intervene, firstly because he was still filled with a deep sense of gratitude for what the lady jackdaw had achieved and secondly because he still found the whole thing wonderfully stirring. News of the heroic exploit had attracted all kinds of birds to the forest clearing and all were listening spellbound, apart from the late arrivals who were so far away from the lady jackdaw that they could catch only the occasional word. As a result they were seething rebelliously at the back.

"What's she say?" they demanded irritably. "Can't hear a word back here. It's ridiculous. Can't someone get her to speak up?"

Unable to ignore these fervent appeals, those nearer the front felt under an obligation to come to the aid of those at the back by turning around and repeating the bit they had just heard. Unfortunately this had the effect of distracting the birds who were in front of them. Finding it difficult to concentrate they started turning round and saying: "Shhhhh" and "Do you mind?" so loudly that the birds who had been selflessly trying to assist by repeating parts of the narrative found it impossible to hear what was being said themselves, with the result that the flow of information to the back was immediately suspended and the original complaints began again with redoubled indignation. Newcomers found themselves being drawn into the dispute on one side or the other and soon the several factions had turned their backs on the lady jackdaw and were contesting the matter among themselves with such fervour that not surprisingly she began to falter. At one point she even stopped talking altogether whereupon the riotous assembly came instantly to order and broke into prolonged and generous applause, under the impression that she had finished her story.

Gazing down upon the turbulent scene, Wake could not help

reflecting that one of the basic requirements of a plan, namely that it be a secret, at least from someone, was being largely overlooked. He was perched on the dilapidated fence surrounding the garden of the ruined cottage. The precious handkerchief was draped across a strand of wire beside him and on the other side his five companions were lined up, waiting for the lady jackdaw to conclude her address, so that the great adventure could begin.

Now it was no mere chance that the swallow sitting next to Wake on the fence was Bony. Without ever being formally invited to assume the role, he was now acting as Wake's second-in-command. He was undoubtedly the largest and the strongest of the little band, a swallow of actions rather than words, only really happy when proceeding in a forward direction, preferably to the sound of cheering. Throughout the confusion of the scene in the clearing he had quite obviously been finding it extremely difficult to conceal his impatience and as the loud and rapturous applause reluctantly subsided at the conclusion of the lady jackdaw's story, Bony decided to bring the proceedings to a close.

"May I?" he murmured. Wake could only nod his head in bemused assent. Bony smiled back re-assuringly and raising his voice addressed the still excited assembly.

"Right then, all you birds, may I please have your attention? Wake wishes me to thank you for your attendance here today and for the interest you have shown. Now he requests that you all disperse quietly while we go and fetch Creakwing and set off for Africa!"

You may well find it almost incredible, now that the whole world knows how appallingly difficult and dangerous the Crossing turned out to be, to reflect that at that stage in the great adventure Wake had given almost no thought to the fine detail of his plan. All that existed in his mind were vague and heroic pictures. In those pictures he seemed to see the orange and yellow handkerchief floating bravely over land and sea, flanked by its gallant escort, with their wounded leader warmly wrapped in its ample folds, and he himself gazing proudly ahead for that first glimpse of the legendary land of Africa where undying fame awaited them all. The detail had eluded him. To be fair, since Creakwing had announced his intention of remaining behind there had not been much time to reflect on these matters and a great deal had already been achieved but now that the lady jackdaw had courageously played her part he was becoming increasingly aware that it was now up to him; important decisions had to be made if they were not to betray all that she had achieved. What these decisions might be he was not exactly sure but what he was clear about was the fact that there was no question of simply bundling Creakwing into the handkerchief and setting off with no further preparation or planning. Bony's announcement was quite ludicrous and had also embarrassed him in front of all the other birds.

He became aware that silence had gradually settled over the colourful assembly, a silence filled with a strange, suppressed excitement, as though they were all waiting for him to bear them up to even greater heights of sensation. Since he had nothing specific in mind Wake could not have been more relieved when the little blue tit came suavely to his rescue. So many birds were now milling about in the forest clearing that he had not even noticed he was there. They had not met since the rather futile experiment in the orchard but the little bird alighted beside him on the fence almost as though he was expected and then with every indication of deep respect addressed himself to Bony, the self-appointed second-in-command.

"Do you mind?"

Bony scowled automatically but so serenely did the little bird return his glare that he edged grudgingly along and made room for the newcomer. Settled alongside Wake the blue tit whispered: "Do you mind if I just take over for a minute? Sort a few things out?" As he spoke Wake could sense something new in his eyes, an extra warmth as though the little bird thoroughly approved of him.

The blue tit had one of those rather quiet voices you really have to strain to listen to but would never dream of interrupting with an observation so impolite as: "Speak up, we can't hear."

"May I have your attention, please?" he announced. The silence grew even more expectant. "My good friend Wake wishes me to express his gratitude and thanks for the interest and support you have shown in coming along here today."

Upon hearing this one or two of the assembled birds shook their heads deprecatingly; others protested that it was the least they could do. The owl said: "Not at all," very loudly. And there was a brief attempt to strike up the avian[14] version of "For He's Jolly Good Fellow."

---

[14] *Avian: Pertaining to birds. From the Latin: Avis, meaning a bird.*

The blue tit raised his little wing and the assembly fell silent once again. "The swallows must now make their final preparations. Time is running short and there is much to be done before they leave." At these words Bony smiled sceptically but the blue tit did not appear to notice. "Once again, on behalf of Wake and the others, may I thank you for your attendance and assure you that you will be kept fully informed of all developments." He turned back to Wake and his manner was almost apologetic. "I do hope you don't mind. I would like to help if I can."

Bony looked mildly aggrieved over the blue tit's intervention in what he clearly considered to be a swallow affair but Wake said simply: "Thank you. We would be grateful for your help."

He could not help reflecting how remarkably pleasant it was to remain silent and grave before a large and attentive assembly while important announcements are made on your behalf. At the same time, as the birds began to disperse from the clearing, he felt an enormous relief. The tit family's reputation for practical intelligence was well-known and the blue tit would undoubtedly be most useful in considering the technical problems associated with the flight.

Every day had brought some new evidence of the strangeness of winter, some disturbing revelation to remind the swallows how desperate their plight had become and the latest evidence of this was there in the field selected by the blue tit for the very first experimental flights of what we will now think of as the sky-boat. Everything had changed; once this place had been alive with the tidal flow of the gleaming corn as it moved in the warm winds of autumn but now it was a vast expanse of frozen stubble, pallid and motionless in the cold, still mist of the winter afternoon and as they alighted on the ground the earth was hard and unyielding under their tiny feet.

The blue tit, however, had chosen the place with care. It was well away from any curious spectators there might be among the bird population and was also the field farthest away from the farm where the swallows lived; it was unlikely that any humans would have any business out there on such a dreary afternoon.

Hence, in English: Aviator, aviation, aviary. Enlightened teachers realising that this book is not without educational merit may wish to purchase a copy or two for the school library at the usual rates.

He had also selected that particular field because it would afford him a good view of the test flight, being wide and open with no trees nearby and sloping gently away from them down towards the estuary.

It was here that the flight tests began under the personal supervision of the blue tit. And just one hour later Wake was in total despair, convinced that after its first real test his plan had come to an end in disaster and humiliation.

It all began, to his great surprise, with the blue tit calling on Bony. In a distinctly friendly way he inquired which of the swallows it was he had heard announcing to the assembly in the forest that they would be leaving immediately. Looking enormously pleased at this early recognition of his sterling qualities, Bony stepped forward.

"Good." The blue tit beamed at him in a most amiable manner. "Would you mind just demonstrating for me how you think we should proceed?"

Bony looked inquiringly at the other swallows. Wake assumed a stern expression; Bess edged a little closer towards him; and Harold, Oliver and Winnie gazed thoughtfully at the ground.

"Just a quick demonstration," suggested the blue tit smoothly and then he looked just a little apprehensive and added: "But please don't go too far. Remember we aren't ready to leave just yet."

"Don't see why not," said Bony stoutly. "We just put him in the middle, lift up the corners and away we go. Next stop Africa. But if that's what you want we'll just go to the end of the field."

"That would be wonderful," said the blue tit with every sign of gratitude. "Now you are going to need some assistance, of course. What about you three?" Winnie, Harold and Oliver glanced imploringly at Wake but he merely nodded his approval of the suggestion, whereupon the reluctant volunteers joined Bony, to form a circle on the ground around the handkerchief.

With a rather intellectual expression on his face, Bony gazed down at the handkerchief for a moment and then he looked up at the blue tit who was perched between Wake and Bess on the top bar of the gate.

"I really need Bess to sit in the handkerchief to make it more real," he explained.

"Oh, don't worry about that, "said the blue tit dismissively. And the panic subsided from Bess's face, as he added: "Just use a bit of soil. It's quite hard. Choose a piece about the same size as Creakwing. But be as quick as you can. It'll be dark soon."

In those few moments since taking charge Bony had assumed an air of confident authority. His resolute manner seemed to indicate that if all went well they would probably be away within the hour. Under his supervision the swallows laid the handkerchief down on a piece of flat ground at the edge of the field. He personally selected a lump of earth approximately the same size as a swallow and helped by the others manoeuvred it into the middle of the handkerchief. Then he ordered a swallow to each corner.

"When I say: 'Lift' I want you to take your corner of the handkerchief in your beak and when I say: 'Fly' I want us all to head off in a southerly direction." He looked at them sternly. "As this is the first flight we will not go beyond the end of the field."

Disaster was almost immediate. Let us say the problem was unforeseen but not unforeseeable. It had not apparently occurred to Bony who had taken up position at the front right hand corner that in order to issue the order to "fly" he would have to open his beak. Because he was not prepared for it his corner of the handkerchief fell out. The result was that the other three swallows rose into the air, leaving him behind on the ground, looking incredibly alone, with his beak still open in surprise. There was no time for him to become lonely, however, for the triumphant progress of his companions was to last for only a moment. Without him the handkerchief was no longer airworthy, if indeed it had ever enjoyed that distinction. The unattached corner draped itself over the heads of the other three swallows, cutting off their view of the end of the field at which they had all been gazing so resolutely; and enveloped in the folds of the handkerchief all three swallows crashed back to earth.

Wake watched his companions struggling to disentangle themselves with mounting irritation but noticed with surprise that the blue tit seemed quite unperturbed by the disaster. He nodded encouragingly at Bony and said: "Once more, if you would. Only this time when you take off I would try to keep hold of the handkerchief."

This time the handkerchief did become airborne but only briefly. The problem was basically one of technique. You will remember that migrating swallows employ a quite different method of flight, the so-called "bounding" motion which ensures not only that the

Crossing takes place in as short a time as possible but also that all the swallows fly more or less in the same direction; the aerial antics of feeding swallows would be quite inappropriate on such a long journey. Unfortunately Bony and his three reluctant volunteers had forgotten the necessity for this kind of flight discipline which was after all quite new to them. They made the vital error of taking off without reaching any firm agreement on the direction in which they intended to go. As the swallows rose from the ground they were in fact following four different courses, approximately WSW, SSW, S and SSE and the handkerchief proved unequal to the challenge. All four corners were snatched from their beaks and as the square of silk floated serenely back to earth the extra velocity experienced by the swallows, as they found themselves suddenly relieved of their burden, sent them hurtling across the sky, in different directions, the distance between them widening all the time, rather like the expansion of the Universe, before they regained control and returned rather sheepishly to the entrance of the field. Wake could not conceal his scorn.

"You can't even fly properly yourselves, so why you think you can fly with the handkerchief I can't imagine."

He could not understand why the blue tit was tolerating such foolishness. If he intended to help them why didn't he do something? But the blue tit seemed quite unaffected by the failure of the experiment. In fact he gave every indication that he had not really taken very much interest in it. Throughout the drama of the two attempts to fly the handkerchief he had been busily engaged in a series of mathematical calculations and even though the flight tests had at times been accompanied by loud cries of alarm and fervent appeals for help he had scarcely looked up from the figures and drawings he was making with his foot in the frosty surface all along the top bar of the gate. Wake saw that some of the drawings resembled the shape of the handkerchief but there were also a great many more little lines and circles he could not begin to understand.

The blue tit worked on, murmuring to himself and occasionally whistling a vague little tune when something he had written proved particularly pleasing. He seemed quite unaware of the slightly restless scrutiny to which he was being subjected, especially by Bony. Soon the whole length of the top of the gate was covered with his calculations and he politely requested Wake and Bess to move along a little to provide a fresh surface on which they could continue. At one point he impatiently expunged a whole sequence of figures and softly chided himself with the words: "They won't want to go backwards, you idiotic bird!" After about half an hour he gave a little sigh of satisfaction and then peered down at Bony and his three companions who were still assembled on the ground in a little group around the handkerchief.

"We're almost there but I wonder if you'd mind just doing again what you did last time?"

Bony looked a little puzzled and glanced at his three co-pilots for enlightenment. They declined to meet his gaze. After two successive mishaps they had clearly transferred their devotion to the blue tit at whom they were gazing with fervent hope.

"Do what again?" demanded Bony.

"What you did before."

"But that wasn't what I was trying to do."

"Well, it wouldn't be, would it?" agreed the blue tit.

"I was in fact trying to do something completely different," added Bony, with just a hint of defiance. "We'll do that if you like."

The blue tit looked deeply gratified. "That would be very helpful," he said and then, appearing to take Bony into his confidence, he murmured: "I'm trying to discover all the things which could go wrong and you, if I may say so, do seem to have a natural gift for that kind of research. You see, there is one other problem which might occur and I believe you could help us to identify it." Bony looked resolute once more and said: "What problem is it?"

"Ah," said the blue tit confidentially, "I would prefer to leave that to you."

This time Bony remembered not to open his beak; all four swallows remembered to adopt the migratory mode of flight, so that they were all heading in the same direction. And in no time at all they had proved the blue tit to be entirely correct in his prediction; there was another problem.

It was not at first apparent. For a few moments the handkerchief rose smoothly through the still, cold air and Wake's heart was lifting with it. Winnie and Harold were stationed at the rear corners with the handkerchief firmly wedged in their beaks and appeared to experience no difficulty. The problem involved Oliver and Bony who, in trying to adopt a similar position at the front corners , were obliged to fly alongside the handkerchief. It proved to be impossible. Each beat of their wings snagged the sides of the handkerchief and after a few seconds Bony called: "Release." And once more the swallows watched in anguish as the handkerchief floated slowly down to drape itself across a furrow just a short distance into the field.

"Good," said the blue tit, as soon as the swallows were all together again. "In fact, excellent." He looked down at Bony and added with enormous warmth: "You and your friends have demonstrated in no fewer than three different ways how it is possible not to fly with the handkerchief. I am deeply grateful. Now, if you'll excuse us, there are a few things I have to discuss with Wake." He beamed down for a moment at the despondent swallows and then almost as an afterthought he added the startling comment: "I estimate that you should be able to leave in about two days from now."

For a long time after the others had gone Wake remained behind with the blue tit. Perched on the top bar of the gate he listened with growing amazement as his friend explained his plan. The blue tits were the only birds in the forest with a tendency to become excited in the presence of sums and in his eagerness to explain the little bird scampered along the top of the gate from one end to the other. Sometimes he seemed positively startled by his own brilliance.[15]

"Quite frankly, I'm amazed," he confessed. "There's never been anything like it before. But I assure you it will fly. I've known for days what the problem would be and there's the answer. What do you think?"

Wake was not good at sums. Not many birds were. As he gazed down at the blue tit's calculations with what he hoped was an extremely intelligent expression, his thoughts were elsewhere. His main emotion, as he reflected on how brilliantly the blue tit had solved the technical problems of flying the handkerchief, was one of relief. This was the moment he had been awaiting with some anxiety; the moment when he had to inform Creakwing of the plan. So far the old leader's illness had meant that it was possible to carry

---

[15] *Bird Brain of Britain, 1985. Independent tests conducted with the full co-operation of the tit family established that in solving practical engineering problems of an often complex nature they were without equal among birds.*

94

on with his preparations without the need for explanations but with their departure now imminent he would have to be told. Nothing less than an intelligent and logical plan would satisfy him; if he felt the idea was rash or foolhardy he would simply refuse to go with them. But the plan was perfect, thanks to this excitable little genius. Wake looked at the blue tit with an expression of deep regard and prepared to say something solemnly appropriate to the occasion, on behalf of swallows everywhere.

"I just want to say---"

"Don't forget," interrupted the blue tit. He was still gazing down admiringly at his sums and did not appear to have appreciated the awesome nature of the moment. "First thing tomorrow, we meet here for the proper flight tests. That's when we'll see if you swallows can learn to fly this thing."

* * *

Chapter 11

For many days now Creakwing had been feeling very odd indeed. To begin with he found it difficult to know if he was very hot or very cold. Sometimes he was one, sometimes the other and sometimes he seemed to be both at the same time. He was also very puzzled by an almost continuous procession of strange and unusual visitors. They were birds of a kind he could not remember ever having seen before, who addressed him in a very unusual way, apart from one who said nothing at all but simply sat a few feet away from him, laughing at the top of his voice. Every time he tried to complain about their behaviour they instantly disappeared. And whenever he tried to puzzle things out he fell asleep.

The morning after the swallows' disastrous experiment with the skyboat he awoke in the barn feeling much better but convinced that the night before he had successfully concluded yet another Crossing. He felt weak but there was nothing unusual about that at the end of such a journey. With a familiar feeling of relief and pride he struggled to the window ledge, expecting to look out upon a landscape bathed in the heat of an African morning and to feel an old delight in the transformation. Instead he was astonished to see that outside the barn everywhere was still and cold and crisp with frost. And then he remembered that the thing he feared most in all the world had come to pass; he was still there in that northern land and winter had come. The thought did not frighten him since he had known for a long time that this had been his last summer. What he did find appalling was the realisation that he was still sharing the barn with these six troublesome swallows. Even more irritatingly, they seemed quite unconcerned about the danger they were in. Quite the reverse, for they appeared to be strangely excited about something.

"Wake will explain," they laughed. "And tell you were to sit."

And Wake did explain, his eyes shining with valour and excitement. As he spoke the old bird found himself much more intrigued by the faces of his companions than by Wake himself. He had seen that expression of trust and respect in the eyes of swallows before; he had even seen it in the faces of swallows as they regarded him; and he knew that such a look was usually reserved for leaders. He could not help wondering what this misguided little bird had been doing to inspire such apparent devotion.

He sensed that it was important not to be too unkind. These swallows had been very foolish. He could hardly bear to think of the anguish they had caused their parents; how many times down there in the haven of their winter home had he watched with sadness as parent birds scanned those empty northern skies for missing offspring who never came? But this was not the time for recriminations. After all these birds were there because of him; he was still responsible for them. And there was just a chance, if the weather did not deteriorate, that they could still reach Africa.

The change he feared most of all was snow. He knew that the cold white carpet he saw now on the ground every morning was not snow but it certainly meant that snow was near. He had only ever glimpsed it at a distance, on the tops of far-away hills and he had no wish to be any closer. He had heard what snow could do to the ability of migrating birds to find their way. If the wind did change direction and the snow fell before these inexperienced swallows set off they might never see Africa.

The vital thing was to get them on their way with no further delay and this ridiculous business with the handkerchief was merely delaying their departure. The first thing he had to do was to ensure that they abandoned the idea. He had now fully accepted that he at least would never see Africa again and he certainly had no intention of being carried there in the middle of a silk handkerchief!

"I'll come and meet your friend," he said, "and I'll hear what he has to say but remember: I am still your leader and if I disapprove of your plan you must obey my orders and leave immediately-- without me."

Creakwing kept his word. Later that morning he accompanied the swallows to the test site in the field above the estuary where the blue tit was already waiting. He had clearly not been idle since the experiment of the day before. Alongside the handkerchief he had assembled a number of curiously-shaped twigs which he had carried to the field before dawn in six separate trips. Perched on the gate beside the blue tit Creakwing tried to concentrate as he began to explain how they would be used but it was difficult. For the first time that morning he had become aware of the snow heaped on the distant hills and found it hard to think of anything else. At last he became aware that a silence had settled on the little gathering and realised with embarrassment that he had not heard the question addressed to him by the blue tit.

"I beg your pardon. I was thinking of something else."

The merest flicker of impatience crossed the little bird's features and he said: "I was expressing the hope that you would not be too uncomfortable since we have to carry a reserve supply."

"Of what?" enquired the old leader.

"Of oars," interrupted Wake and the old leader could tell that he, too, was annoyed with him. It was time to end this pointless business and get the swallows on their way.

"Look," he said, with less than total honesty, "I've listened to what you have to say. I admire all the thought and preparation you have put into your plan. But we have no time now to get involved in this sort of thing. You've seen the snow this morning. You swallows have to get going now, today, if you're going to have any chance at all. Even so it's not going to be easy for you."

Creakwing was confidently anticipating the response he had observed many times in the past whenever it became necessary to rebuke younger birds for challenging his authority but this time his air of kindly severity failed to achieve the expected response. He was rather taken aback to see six swallows gazing back at him with identical expressions in which respect was most noticeably absent.

"I don't quite understand," said Wake icily. "We are now ready to leave. We are not asking you to *do* anything, just to come with us."

Creakwing felt a pang of shame; his response to this plan which clearly meant a great deal to the young swallows had been less than generous.

"What Wake means is that it hasn't been easy," said the blue tit diplomatically. "A great many birds have been involved in this plan right from the beginning and some of them have taken enormous risks." Creakwing gazed down at the handkerchief with its yellow and orange pattern.

"Risks?"

The blue tit began to relate the events of the past few weeks, as the old swallow listened with growing amazement. The little bird's manner was mild enough but Creakwing could tell from the fierce concentration of the swallows as they listened to his words how proud they were of what had been achieved. He felt humbled by the knowledge that all these things had been happening on his behalf. The blue tit told the story of Wake's visit to the jackdaws in the centre of the forest without embellishment but he knew at once what it must have involved to make such a journey alone in the middle of the night with such a request. That was impressive enough but the revelation of the jackdaw's valour in entering the house of a human family to seize this infernal handkerchief was almost unbelievable.

"Don't forget the little yellow bird," reminded Bess.

"The little yellow bird?"

The blue tit nodded to her to continue and Bess took up the story. Sweet Bess who felt everything so deeply was still clearly upset about the little yellow bird who could never fly south. Unusually for her she concluded her story with a gentle reproach.

"He knew that he could never leave," she said, "but he wanted you to have the chance and he was even prepared to lose the trust of his human family to ensure that you could go."

"There is one other thing," said Wake. "The blue tit hasn't mentioned his own part in the plan; all the sums he had to do." He turned to the little bird. "Perhaps you could explain."

Could the blue tit explain? His deepest joy in life was explanations and he made it an invariable rule always to start at the beginning and never to take any short cuts on his way to the end; repetitions were also freely available.

"Basically, "he began, "we were faced with a problem of aerodynamics and aerodynamics as you know is the science of flight......"

It was the first really complicated explanation that Creakwing had ever suffered and he found the experience distinctly unnerving. Every time he backed away a little to increase the space between them the explanation simply followed him along the top of the gate. If he appeared to encourage it by nodding in an intelligent sort of way it became even more excited and if he shook his head admiringly and said: "Well, I'm blowed," it grew appreciably louder and actually jumped up and down. In the end he decided to do nothing further to provoke it and waited as patiently as possible for it to end.

"So you see," said the blue tit triumphantly at last, "the skyboat will fly. All we have to do now is to teach the swallows how to fly it."

Creakwing felt bewildered. So much had been happening without his knowledge. Always before he had been at the centre of things; few important decisions were taken until he had been consulted. And yet in this important matter he had been unable to assist or even advise. In another sense, though, he was right at the centre of what had been happening because he was the reason for the astonishing activities which had brought them to this moment, out there in a cold and silent landscape under a sky laden with snow.

He glanced around at the six youngsters, huddled together and shivering in the frosty air, as they awaited his response. What a terrible state they were in, far too thin with their plumage matted and dirty. Did they know how strange they looked, these winter swallows? He looked down at the handkerchief. It lay open on the ground, like a flag waiting to be raised, and in all that frozen waste the only sign of warmth was the great yellow sun blazing away in the centre of it. His gaze took in the pathetic little stack of hawthorn twigs lying beside it. The whole idea was quite absurd, a childish fantasy but this was probably not the time to say so; events would prove him right.

"All right." He had regained a little of his old authority. "We will try it but we must agree on one thing. I shall be in command and if I think the plan has become impossible you must abandon it and go on alone."

Rather to Creakwing's surprise his generous concession did not meet with the relief and gratitude he had expected.

"I am very sorry, Creakwing," said Wake, "but the swallows will be under my orders. I will lead the way."

Six pairs of eyes awaited his reaction. The blue tit paused in the task of sorting through the hawthorn twigs but did not look up. In the silence Creakwing contemplated Wake with his old severity as though daring him to continue.

"Once we set out we will do our best to carry you all the way but if anything goes wrong.".…. Here Wake hesitated. "If anything happens to you, my friends here will still need a leader to get them through, so it is better that I lead from the beginning."

Creakwing regarded him in a thoughtful sort of way. This young swallow had certainly changed since the summer. He was much more proud and difficult but was he proud and difficult enough to be a leader?

"So you want to lead from the beginning?" he murmured. "Perhaps you will tell me how you plan to do so, since you have never crossed before and presumably do not know the way."

The wise and experienced Creakwing had questioned many swallows who aspired to be leaders. He knew the nature of the response he was seeking and he was not dissatisfied with this one. Even though it was delivered in a bemused sort of way.

"I know I've never crossed before," confessed the little swallow, "and I know I can't possibly know the way. But the funny thing is.... I keep thinking I will remember it."

* * *

Chapter 12

Before we embark upon this chapter allow me, if I may, to offer my assurances that although it does appear at first sight to contain material of a mathematical nature which could prove disturbing to children of a nervous disposition things are not what they seem. It is undeniably true that the following pages do include several diagrams with little arrows leading off from them, to a series of capital letters, but you have my word as an Englishman that you will find no algebra, geometry or any other kind of harmful mathematics anywhere in the pages which follow. Nor will this material form the basis of any test, examination or verbal grilling. I am well aware that writing books with sums in is no way to make friends but I am afraid the story must now become a little technical to allow me to illustrate exactly how the blue tit converted the handkerchief into a skyboat. This little bit will soon be over and you will enjoy the rest of the story all the more if you now sit up straight and pay attention.

One of the truly astonishing things about the whole adventure was Wake's failure to appreciate the technical problems of such a flight. From the beginning he had been so carried along by his own heroic thoughts (and indeed by the admiration of other birds) that he gave scarcely any thought to these matters. He had not objected when Bony and the others made their first attempt to fly because he assumed that was the way it would have to be done. The failure of that first flight had caused him great embarrassment. That little square of brightly coloured silk was the visible symbol of their great adventure; a great deal had already been risked to secure it. And the first time it had been put to use it had crashed ignominiously to the ground after just a few yards. Luckily for them, however, the blue tit, with his scientific turn of mind, had thought about the problem very carefully indeed. He very quickly appreciated that the main difficulty would be to ensure that the swallows were able to carry the handkerchief without at the same time becoming entangled in it, not just to the end of the field but all the way across vast distances he could hardly begin to comprehend, all the way to the place the swallows called Africa.

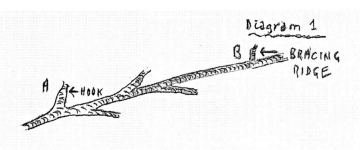

Diagram 1

B ← BRACING RIDGE

A ←HOOK

Before trimming

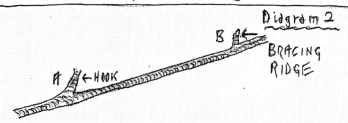

Diagram 2

B ← BRACING RIDGE

A ←HOOK

After trimming

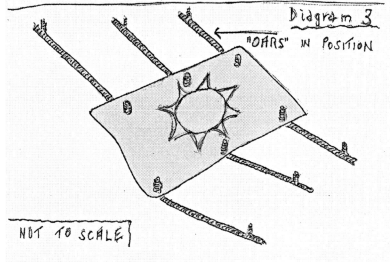

Diagram 3

← "OARS" IN POSITION

NOT TO SCALE

The use of the twigs really was a stroke of genius and it is my opinion that only a member of the tit family could have thought of it.[16] It was a brilliantly simple solution to the problem. That little stack of twigs lying beside the handkerchief might have given the impression of having been taken quite at random from the hawthorn tree but in fact they were all alike in a very special way, carefully selected by a team of volunteers from the blue tit's family, according to his very precise instructions.

In Diagram (1) I have shown one of them in the rough state before it was adapted according to the blue tit's instructions. What I want you to note particularly are the features marked A and B. All the twigs had these features in common although of course none of them was identical. The feature marked A we shall call the hook and B the lifting point. Diagram (2) shows how the twigs looked after they had been adapted for flight by trimming.

The blue tit's plan was to use six of these twigs, very much in the manner of a boat's oars to convert the handkerchief for flight. The resemblance to oars was really only in appearance, though, because their function was quite different; by using them instead of their beaks to lift the handkerchief the swallows were able to control it in flight whilst remaining far enough away to ensure their wings could be fully extended.

In converting the handkerchief into a skyboat it had also been necessary to damage it by cutting six small holes, three on each side and exactly opposite each other (a fact which was to create an enduring mystery for humans in the years to come, as you will learn later). The end of the oar marked A in Diagram (2) was carefully inserted in each of these holes with the hook pointing upwards leaving them securely fixed and protruding sideways from the handkerchief, as in Diagram (3).

There was one additional feature I should draw your attention to. It was concerned with the weather conditions the swallows were

---

[16] *In fact, the principle was later to be incorporated into the basic engineering course which was compulsory for all young tits. It was used to illustrate the principle that a complicated problem could be solved in a simple way using materials lying immediately to hand. In later years the blue tit himself was to be heaped with all kinds of academic honours for his idea, including the tit family equivalent of the Nobel prize for Science.*

likely to encounter on their journey. During his calculations the blue tit had worked out that in severe weather the skyboat was quite likely to become unstable. Heavy rain could soak into the fabric and increase its weight and in unusually high winds the square of silk was quite likely to start functioning like a sail. To cope with these contingencies he had stipulated that the twigs should be selected with an outgrowth at the lifting point marked B. This was then trimmed back to form a slight ridge at the end of the oar. With their beaks grasping the oar on the inner side of this ridge and braced against it the swallows were less likely to have the oars torn from their beaks in severe weather conditions.

That was the theory of the skyboat which was now to be put to the test. The six swallows and the blue tit gathered in exactly the same spot in which their first attempts to fly the handkerchief had failed so ignominiously. Creakwing was not present. With a rather weary air he had asked to be excused, saying that he was perfectly content to leave it all to them.

If the blue tit was nervous he did not show it. "For this first test we will use just four of the oars," he instructed. "In that way Bess can play the part of Creakwing and Wake and I can observe from the gate and identify any problems."

Wake watched from his vantage point at the top of the gate as Bess sank down nervously in the middle of the handkerchief.

"Right in the middle," fussed the blue tit. "You must be exactly in the middle at all times or the balance won't be right. Before you set off I must remember to mark the centre with a cross just to remind Creakwing where to sit."

Gravely Bony and his three companions moved to their positions. The four oars had been hooked through the holes at the corners leaving the two central ones empty and by some oversight Harold and Winnie took up position at the front. "Excuse me," said Bony primly and with a muttered apology they moved to the rear. Bony took possession of the right hand oar and waved Oliver into place beside the other one. "I will lead," he announced.

"If you will permit me," corrected the blue tit, "there will be no leaders. You must fly as one. That is the most important thing of all. You must all do the same thing at the same time or it will not fly."

Wake saw with concern that little Bess looked very nervous indeed. Her tiny feet were clutching the fabric beneath her and she kept adjusting her position. From time to time she glanced apprehensively at the long oars leading out from the edge of the handkerchief to the four waiting swallows. He realised the reason for her concern. If the skyboat reached a good height and then something went wrong her wings could not save her if she was tangled in the silk folds of the handkerchief as it fell back to earth.

"It'll be all right, " he said.

"I know," she agreed and smiled in a doomed sort of way.

The blue tit turned to Wake in a grave and momentous manner. "You give the signal."

Wake glanced down at the orange and yellow handkerchief. How flimsy it looked for such a great enterprise. For a moment his confidence faltered and although his smile was unconcerned it was with a sinking heart that he finally gave the order for take-off. He could hardly bear to watch as the four swallows bent forward and picked up the oars, clamping them firmly in their beaks, up against the inside edge of the little ridges. At least they had remembered that much. A quick adjustment and they were ready. Bony paused heroically. Wake resisted the temptation to shout to him to get on with it.

"On the count of three," said Bony. "One.. two". An awesome pause.. "three."

Slowly and awkwardly the skyboat rose from the frozen earth. When only a little distance above the level of the gate it seemed to falter and lurch sideways. Wake drew in his breath but the blue tit showed no emotion. A quick adjustment and the skyboat levelled out. It began to rise higher. Bess was now clinging on desperately because the handkerchief was stretched too tightly. She was in danger of rolling to the edge and falling out but Bony had noticed what was happening. He shouted a warning and they all closed in. The handkerchief hollowed out in the centre under Bess's weight and she sank down again, cushioned in its folds.

There was one awful moment when it seemed to the watchers on the ground that the little craft must crash. For some reason the steady beat of those four pairs of wings became unsynchronised. As three of the swallows surged forward with open wings, Oliver's wings were still closed. Despite the bracing ridge the oar was torn from his beak and with a loud squeal of surprise he fluttered away to one side. With one oar hanging down the skyboat was suddenly unstable. It veered to one side and downwards but Oliver had now recovered and was chasing after it. There was a brief struggle as he fought to retrieve his oar and then he took up position again at the front and once more the little craft was under their control.

As that first demonstration flight went on it seemed at times as though the handkerchief was both alive and malicious, determined not to yield to them. It sought to confuse them by constantly changing its shape. It tried to snatch the oars from their beaks with quick impatient movements. But all the time their power to control it was growing until at last came the moment when the skyboat seemed to surrender and finally acknowledge the swallows' authority. And then the watchers on the ground saw that it was leaping through the air, as a boat surges forward through the sea. On the upbeat the wings of the swallows closed together and on the downbeat they opened, carrying them and the skyboat forward in a long, gliding motion. The key to their success was their obvious and absolute mastery of this migratory method of flying. The erratic brilliance of summer flight had gone. Now they flew soberly in the new way, the way they had been taught in preparation for the Crossing. So quickly did they master this new technique that in a very short time the skyboat had reached a great height.

The swallows flew as one, responding instinctively to the smallest ripple of movement in the silk square. They seemed to know when to be strong and resist and when to appear to weaken and give way. If a violent surge of wind caught their little craft they went with it, banking across the sky and slowly taking back control as the wind subsided but if the movement was slight enough to be resisted they tightened their grip and refused to yield.

It was almost as though the four swallows had merged into one. Their different thoughts and feelings ran like nerves, up the length of the oars and out across that billowing surface, connecting them to each other and to something even larger than themselves. They were for ever altered by the experience of that first flight. They were no longer the kind of swallows who liked to lounge about watching others do things. They had found something they could do supremely well which no one had ever done before.

Like a banner that bright and flowing swirl of silk crossed the winter sky. Many other birds saw it go and never forgot what they had seen, nor the strange little shivers they had felt as it passed overhead. They talked of it off and on until their dying day and many insisted that what they had witnessed was not a training flight at all but the actual departure, so stirring had they felt the sight to be.[17]

The swallows had traversed the first field and were heading down across the second, on their way towards the estuary when the blue tit at last broke the silence. Without taking his eyes off the dwindling shape of the skyboat he remarked mildly that perhaps Wake had better go and bring them back.

"It would be a great pity if they flew all the way to Africa with Creakwing still here."

The next task was to test the efficiency of the skyboat with all six oars in operation and here Wake found himself becoming just a little irritated by the attitude of Bony and his companions. The start of the second test flight was delayed for some minutes because three of the original test pilots--Bony, Oliver and Harold-- were still swaggering about like veterans of some awesome adventure, indulging in loud and unlikely recollections for the benefit of Winnie whose interest and admiration did her great credit, since you will remember that she had actually taken part in the events they were describing.

Once more the flight went well and this time they were able to establish that the role of the two central oars was quite different from that of the oars situated at the corners. Their sole function seemed to be to help support the weight of the skyboat, with the oars at the corners controlling such vital functions as course, altitude and speed; or as Wake, who was not familiar with aeronautical procedure thought of it, where they were going, how high they were going and how fast they were going.

It was after that second successful flight that Wake had to re-assert his authority. This became necessary because an unfortunate impression seemed to be developing that Bony was now the leader,

---

[17] *In the years to come when the Winter Crossing had become a much-loved story there was a game young swallows loved to play in the breezy days of Summer if they chanced upon a discarded scrap of material which resembled the handkerchief. They would pretend to re-enact the original flight. Each of them would assume the role of one of the six famous swallows; some of them would even become quite proficient but for them it remained only a game and at the end of it they all went home to their mothers.*

simply because he was flying at the front. He had started insisting that they ought to leave immediately.

"We know we can fly the handkerchief. We've proved it. So let's go now. There's snow coming. Some of the resident birds told me they can smell it. So why don't we get on our way before it comes?" Wake was tempted. He, too, had heard the rumours of snow. According to the birds who knew about winter the wind was turning. It was now coming more often from the east and soon the snow which had fallen on the hills would be falling on the lower ground around the estuary. But this was not his main concern. He considered it was much more important to devote a little more time to perfecting their flying skills. It was ridiculous to contemplate setting out on a journey of such magnitude after just two flight tests. To his relief the blue tit agreed and Bony was effectively silenced. Not only did the blue tit agree, he also devised a way of putting their newly acquired technique to the test, by simulating a series of emergencies and assessing how they coped with them.

For this series of tests he himself took the role of Creakwing, sitting imperturbably in the centre of the handkerchief, coolly calling out instructions and hanging on tightly as the little craft cavorted about the sky. He made them soar upwards, so steeply that it seemed the handkerchief must turn over; then dive towards the ground in an almost vertical descent, straightening out at the very last moment. This, he airily confided, was to see if he could be induced to fall out. They flew with one oar hanging free; then two; and abandoning yet another one established to the blue tit's apparent satisfaction that four oars was the absolute minimum with which the skyboat could be expected to stay aloft.

The final test had the swallows regarding each other with troubled eyes as they thought about it. But the blue tit insisted. For several minutes they flew steadily upwards into the wintry sky until they were higher than they had ever been before and then he ordered them to release all three oars down one side of the handkerchief. As he fell out he kept his wings tightly closed to simulate the action of a crippled bird and began falling helplessly back to earth. Just when it seemed he must hit the ground he pretended to recover and began ascending again in an awkward, fluttering motion. At the same time the swallows who had recovered their oars began diving to meet him. They positioned themselves precisely below the struggling bird and then rose up and scooped him safely into the folds of the handkerchief. They practised this hazardous and spectacular rescue manoeuvre several times before he was completely satisfied. But, as you will discover, the disaster which actually befell the skyboat, very much later, was quite different from any of these and totally unexpected.

At last the blue tit seemed satisfied that no more could be done. The swallows had demonstrated not only that they could fly the skyboat but also that they could continue to control it even in an emergency. Panting slightly from their exertions the little band gathered around the handkerchief in the gloom of that wintry afternoon as the chilling mist came down again, isolating them in their little corner of the field. Wake looked across at the blue tit and their eyes met. How strange it was to reflect, now the time had come for them to leave, that this little bird who had become so much a part of their lives in recent weeks would not be coming with them. Something in the blue tit's eyes told him that he understood these thoughts but he merely grinned in that dismissive way of his and said: "Tomorrow then."

* * *

Chapter 13

Do you know the feeling when you are about to leave somewhere for somewhere else and the place you are leaving is quite all right but you are so excited that you cannot bear the thought of staying there a single minute more? Of course you do. And so you can understand the impatience the swallows were feeling, now that the time had finally come for them to leave.

In the case of the swallows, though, that impatience had also been intensified by a deep foreboding, as a result of a change in the weather. During the night the rusty iron bird on the roof of the barn had turned right round towards the east and by morning the wind was blowing steady and cold in a way they had never experienced before. Soon after dawn the first flakes of snow began to wander up and down a quiet, grey sky in a sheepish sort of way as though they knew they were just a little too early. And as the swallows felt that unfamiliar wetness on their faces they were aware of a new and urgent desire to be gone from that dreadful place.

The change in the weather seemed to have created a new mood among the birds which had stayed behind, a mood almost of desperation. Wake had always believed that when winter finally came it would find the resident birds well-prepared. And yet he could see they, too, were anxious and afraid in a way he had never seen before. The problem of finding food seemed to be their main concern. Wake and the others had been vaguely hungry for so long now that they had almost become used to the feeling. But now the resident birds also seemed pre-occupied with the search for food. At the same time, though, he felt comforted by this deterioration in the weather because it confirmed his belief that even though the attempt to rescue Creakwing was a risky enterprise there really was no alternative.

In those final hours before departure an event occurred which seemed quite extraordinary to Wake in view of the fact that weather conditions were deteriorating so rapidly. It happened towards the end of the morning of that final day. With the time for departure so close he had begun to worry about the possibility of the handkerchief being discovered and decided that it needed to be concealed in a safe place, as far away from the farmhouse as possible. It had been taken under his supervision to the ruins in the middle of the forest and he was still there, passing the time by chatting idly to the jackdaws and his friend the blue tit, when it happened.

The cold in the upper air was now so intense that few birds were flying. Those which did hurried across the sky, swiftly and silently, as close to the ground as possible, in their anxiety to be home. So the last thing Wake was expecting to hear from high above him in the wintry air was the sound of birds. He looked up.. and fell silent. The strange honking sound, like nothing he had ever heard before, was coming from a whole flock of birds. They were incredibly high, higher than he had ever seen birds flying before, even higher than the swifts he had marvelled at in summer. They were strung out in a long line across the sky with a sort of arrowhead formation at the front and very clearly going somewhere. And in their wild and angry commotion it seemed to Wake that there was a warning to him and to all others who might be watching, a warning to stay clear of them.

In silence, he watched them as they passed over the woods, still maintaining that perfect line, deviating neither to left nor right and filling the wide morning with their savage sound, until they disappeared from sight behind the trees. Wake waited for a moment, gazing upwards in the faint expectation that this remarkable occurrence might be repeated but the sky remained empty. He turned to the blue tit.

"What," he implored, "was that?"

"Geese," said the blue tit. "They're heading for the pond. They come here every year from the far north where I hear the winters are even worse." He looked a little puzzled. "They're very late this year, though."

Since everything about winter was a mystery to the swallows Wake had never realised before that there were birds which came from farther to the north seeking refuge from the weather. He found it hard to imagine a place where winter was even worse than it was now around the estuary but the geese had travelled from such a place; and what he and the blue tit had just observed was not the start of their migration but the end of it. It was a chilling reminder that the ordeal which for many birds was now over had yet to begin for them.

Even though the arrival of the geese had served to increase his foreboding he decided to stick to his original plan and wait until dusk before departing. One reason was to spare Creakwing's feelings. It had occurred to him that the old leader might find the manner of their departure embarrassing. He who had guided the swallows away from this place on so many occasions, at the head of a vast throng of followers, would be leaving this time under very different circumstances. It would be kinder to leave as the light was fading when the chances were that there would be fewer birds to observe them. (As you will discover, in this Wake was to be greatly mistaken.)

The other reason for delaying their departure was the need for caution. Never before in the history of the swallows had a migration begun so late. Already there were signs that they were starting to attract attention; not from other birds but from Man. In the past few days there had been worrying reports of an increase in sightings of humans in the lanes and paths around the farm and it seemed it was the winter swallows they were interested in.[18]

As those final hours went by Wake began to feel very serious. He found his thoughts returning to the long and happy days of summer and how different their lives had once been. It occurred to him that it would be rather nice to say his farewells to the birds which had been his companions in those days which now seemed so long ago. He also had a vague idea that if anything unfortunate did happen it would be nice to leave them with pleasant memories of the sort of swallow he had been.

He decided to call first at the pond where the duck lived. There were two reasons for going there; the first was to say good-bye to his old friend; the second was connected with the arrival of the mysterious geese from the north. Seeing that raucous procession crossing the sky had given him an idea. There was one problem connected with the coming migration which up to now he had quite deliberately refused to think about but now it was intruding into his thoughts more and more as nightfall approached and there was just a chance that the leader of the geese from the far north would be able to help.

Wake was astonished to see the change in the pond. It was now completely frozen over and stretched away as far as he could see, flat and still in the bright, low light of the winter morning. Here and there close in to shore the smooth surface was littered with pieces

---

[18] *Bird watchers, of course. But the swallows had nothing to fear from these essentially gentle creatures.*

of wood and small stones which had become embedded in the ice. The little waves had gone and so had the watery, windy sound they used to make. The reeds which once had leaned and swayed and raced the cloud shadows all along the edges of the pond stood motionless now, locked in their icy shackles. The only sign of life appeared to be right out in the middle of that frozen waste where one or two very young gulls were walking about above the water, wondering how to get in! Then he noticed that one small area of the pond was still defying the power of the ice. Over to his left and close in to the bank he saw the glint of open water. All the birds which lived on the pond seemed to have gathered there, including the ducks.

"Well, look who's here," said his friend of the summer. "It's the famous swallow." He turned to his companions. "We are indeed honoured," But his eyes were just as friendly as they had always been. Wake still found it hard to think of anything to say when his fame was mentioned so he ignored the remark and said: "I was just wondering if the geese arrived safely."

"They're over there," said the duck, "but I wouldn't bother going over there if I were you."

The geese were all together, quietly feeding in the grasses along the fringes of the pond. Frost still clung to their bodies and around their faces from their long, high journey and they looked exhausted. They were much bigger than he had imagined, an aloof little group, grim and unsmiling.

"They're not very friendly," whispered the duck. "Don't know why. We try but they just don't seem to want to know. They seem to think they're superior to us because they come from the north." Wake had found himself screwing up the courage to do things so many times in the last few weeks that now he did it automatically. "I have to talk to them," he said.

The leader of the geese was an enormous bird with a startlingly white forehead. It is doubtful if he had ever seen a swallow before but he showed no interest when Wake flew down. Standing so close to this mysterious bird from the north with his cold, steady eyes, a stranger who made no effort to put him at ease, Wake found it hard to arrange his thoughts into their proper order. And when he started to explain who he was, the goose leader made him feel even more uncomfortable.

"I know who you are." He gestured in a dismissive sort of way at the resident birds crowded into the clear waters at the edge of the pond. "This lot have done nothing but talk about you since we got here. Garrulous lot. What do you want with me, boy?" The goose leader's claim to know all about him finally removed what little composure Wake possessed. He had been planning to relate the whole story but clearly that was no longer necessary. He decided to point out merely that he was the leader of the little group of swallows but had never made a Crossing before let alone led one and would appreciate a little chat. The goose winced at the prospect of such cosiness but listened without comment as Wake explained his dilemma. And then he seemed to lose patience.

"Have you any idea what the weather is going to be like around here very soon now?" Wake did not reply. "We've just battled through some of the worst weather I've ever seen," the goose continued. "Fog, snow, gales, we've had the lot. We should have been here ages ago. That weather is heading this way and you haven't even gone yet. I don't give much for your chances."

"We are going tonight," said Wake with spirit. "I just wanted some advice before we go."

The goose said nothing but in that implacable gaze there did seem a faint invitation to continue so once more Wake embarked upon a familiar question; the question which Creakwing had seemed so reluctant or unable to answer. How was he to know the way? The goose listened without expression and when Wake had finished pity appeared in his eyes for a moment and was gone and when at last he spoke his voice was imperceptibly softer.

"You say you are the leader of these unfortunate swallows?" Wake nodded. "Then you must know that the answer lies up there." He gestured up into the wintry sky. "If you are truly a leader you will find your pathway up there. There will be a way through the stars for you, as there was for us in coming here. But since your stars are not my stars I cannot help you; you must find it for yourself." And then the warmth went from his eyes like a light going off. "Now leave me in peace boy. I'm tired and I want to rest."

Wake had one more call to make before leaving. Earlier in the morning his friend the gull had sent word that he would be honoured if the swallows' leader could spare the time to drop in for a brief chat before departure. He had something to tell him which might just prove useful, the message added.

His route to the estuary where the gull was expecting him took Wake over the rookery for the first time since the main migration of the swallows and he was shocked to see how much it had changed. The rooks' nests were now clearly visible in the high, bare branches. One or two were completely wrecked and obviously abandoned and some had disappeared altogether. All of them appeared to have suffered damage. But of the rooks themselves there was no sign.

Conscious that the dim red sun was already sinking lower in the sky he hurried on until he found himself flying over a large field and there he found the rooks. The field was still covered with the ragged stalks of a recently gathered crop and the rooks were down there among them, strung out across the field and all pecking away in a dispirited sort of way. There was no time remaining for farewells so with a pang of regret he sped across the field without stopping. As he did so he glanced down to see if he could recognise any of them. This proved to be impossible; he was far too high. But all at once the rooks below looked up and saw him. He could hear them clearly, cawing excitedly among themselves with their harsh chiming call and then when he was almost at the edge of the field, to his enormous embarrassment, a doleful cheer, distinctly hoarser than he remembered, rose up from the shivering ranks below and saluted him.

As he arrived at the estuary a strange and inexplicable wailing sound was just dying away. He could not imagine where it was coming from but it did not seem to be worrying the gulls. They were roosting on a grassy mound a few yards out from the estuary shore. To his relief he saw that there was no sign of the sea. Ever since he had first discussed with the gulls the nature of the sea he had been firmly of the opinion that he would not even look at it if at all possible.

But his friend the gull had other ideas. "Sit you down," he instructed. "If you've got a few minutes there is something I'd like you to see before you go."

The gulls were roosting in the stunted saltgrass, crouched down as low as they could get, all facing the same way, with their backs to the seaward end of the estuary and their heads pointing into the bitter easterly wind. As he joined them on the ground his friend signalled to the gulls and grinning with anticipation they moved in to form a circle around him, still with their faces into the wind but now completely shielding him from the icy blast.

"I know your feathers aren't really up to this sort of thing," explained the gull. Wake sank back into that warm and breathing blanket feeling warmer than he had felt for days. An observer noting the fact that all the gulls had their backs to him might have gained the impression that he had just said something enormously insulting, for which they were now awaiting an apology, but the stance they had adopted meant that Wake could now see right down the estuary in perfect comfort. His friend joined him inside the protective screen.

"I've asked you to come here because something is about to happen that I want you to see," said his friend. Wake gazed away down the estuary. All he could see were the empty sands and a wide expanse of saltmarsh, flat and unbroken. On this, far away in the distance, a dog was working sheep. As he watched, the last stragglers scampered up to the top of a high grassy embankment running along the edge of the shore, leaving the estuary empty and silent in the failing light of the winter afternoon. What, he wondered, could possibly happen in such a place?

"The noise you heard was the warning they give to humans to leave the sands. It means there is going to be a high tide. It's something I think you ought to see."

Sheltered though he was from the main force of the wind Wake felt the moment when the air started to grow colder. Then, far away down the empty channel, there was movement. Something had emerged from the mist and was coming towards them. It was hard to see clearly but whatever was approaching was wide enough to completely fill the estuary. A long, unbroken ridge of light reaching from shore to shore was rushing towards them, terrible in its silence. Again the air drifted cold against his face. Nervously he flexed his wings. On it surged, the line of its advance marked by the seabirds out on the sandbanks, as they stirred and rose languidly into the air. Closer and closer it came and now he saw that it was a single mighty wave, a wave rippling with foam and trembling with a voracious glee, as those wide, wet lips gobbled up the gleaming sands. Like some great blind beast oblivious of their presence the wave swept past them on the seaward side in a secret whisper of water and continued on up the estuary.

Now that the sea had gone past without touching their grassy island Wake began to relax. Standing beside him his friend the gull seemed to sense his relief.

"Wait."

In the silence Wake felt his apprehension starting to return. For a moment nothing happened and then when it did it was so unexpected and gave him so much relief and pleasure that he almost laughed out loud. All round the grassy knoll on which the birds were assembled there were other little raised islands of grass just like theirs, stretching out from the line of the shore. Between them lay the shining sands and what he had just noticed was a gentle trickle of water emerging quietly into view from behind one of these little mounds. It was the first, humble emissary of the mighty sea.[19] As he watched, it came meandering towards them across the sands, feeling its way forward, first pausing, then rushing, just like a small and nervous animal.

With equal diffidence, from around the other side, another little stream now appeared. Almost as though they had suddenly sensed each other's presence they seemed to increase their speed and a moment later they were blending in an excited swirl of water immediately below him. Everywhere he looked the waters were uniting in this way. Now the grassy mounds were true islands, isolated amid deepening brown water flecked with foam. Farther out from the shore in the main channel where only a moment ago everything had been so still and quiet there was now only movement and commotion. The sea was full and deep, swirling and turning in all directions as though confused by the suddenness of its own triumph. Borne on the tide a whole tree trunk went surging past. Already it seemed to Wake that there was far too much of it for that narrow place but still from somewhere out in the mist the sea poured in. Finally the waves were massed from shore to shore, jostling and pushing, their crests streaming like banners in the strengthening wind and at the same time from the throat of the sea came a sound like exultation.

---

[19] *It is said, and I have no reason to disbelieve it, that for just two moments every day, far out in the oceans of the world, the sea forgets its terrible anger and during those brief interludes everything is calm and quiet as it listens to the waves clamouring for the honour of leading the tide ashore. The chosen wave which comes surging up the estuaries of our rivers announcing the sea is called the tidal bore. This is what Wake observed and you should try to see one, too, for it is truly a mighty sight.*

Looking out for the first time in his life upon that awful sight Wake had the strangest feeling that the sea was alive; not only alive but aware of him and his plan. At that moment as though to confirm these thoughts the sea welled over the edge of the grassy mound and began seeping through the grass towards them. Unhurriedly, the gulls began to stir and the birds which had been shielding him from the wind stood up and stretched and began to move away towards the centre of their shrinking domain.

"You have now seen the power of the sea," said his friend. "But remember that this is only a very small part of it. The sea that you must cross is even more powerful than this. We have nothing to fear from the sea because we are always close to the land but for birds like you it is different. It is said that sometimes on the Crossing birds grow tired. They sink down into the sea and are never seen again." Wake shivered. Had the gull invited him here in order to frighten him?

The gull continued: "Tonight you will be leaving here to attempt a crossing of the sea in winter. That is why we asked you here this afternoon. We have something to tell you. A secret of the sea not usually told to swallows."

The little island was now almost covered in a pool of water, so shallow that the grass beneath still showed clearly through but the gulls were listening intently and did not move.

"There is a story. Even we do not know if it is true." He pointed away down the tumbling wastes of the evening tide. "It tells of a bird which lives out there. In the sea. Few have ever seen it but it is said that it has sometimes been of help to birds like you who try to cross the oceans of the world." The expression in his eyes was unexpectedly gentle as he added: "I thought you and your friends might like to know that if something does go wrong out there you might not be quite as alone as you think. As I say it is only a story but I have heard it many times. Perhaps it is true."

* * *

119

Chapter 14

"I presume that you are equipped with a map. No journey should ever be undertaken without the aid of a large-scale map. And since you will be travelling over the sea which, I am told, is changing all the time, I would advise a map which is as up-to-date as possible."

With mounting concern the owl had waited at home in the forest for the summons to go to the place where the swallows were assembling for departure, in order to "say a few words". The summons had not come. Assuming that in the excitement of the last-minute preparations this important matter had been overlooked he had turned up anyway. Happily the anxiety occasioned by the absence of a map was confined to the owl himself and no general panic ensued but since he had raised the question of the route to be followed I think it would be instructive to spend these final moments before departure reminding ourselves about the awesome journey which is about to begin.

This was the situation in the gathering gloom of that winter afternoon. The swallows were setting out for a land which only one of them had ever seen, on a journey so long that winter lay at one end and summer at the other, and time itself changed along the way. The only reason they dared to make the journey was because they believed in the idea of a pathway running through the night and through the day, a pathway which the clouds could not hide and the winds could not disturb, their only route to the south, the swallows' way, carved by custom for thousands of miles through the empty air of those high places, with only the ghostly memory of those who had gone before, to keep them company along the way.

The only difference was that those other swallows had always made the Crossing in great numbers, drifting south in twittering clouds in the warm and pleasant haze of autumn with experienced leaders at the front. Wake and his band were leaving alone in the depths of winter burdened by a leader who could not fly. And there was an additional complication. For the moment at least they could not rely on Creakwing for advice. This became clear when they returned to the barn for the last time with the skyboat in order to move him across to the place where the jackdaws lived. They arrived to discover the old leader sleeping fitfully again in his nest under the beam. His fever had returned and he was once more too bewildered to have any idea what was happening.

The clearing in the forest was now bustling with last-minute activity. The handkerchief had been stretched out on the grass in front of the ruined cottage and under the blue tit's supervision the oars were being fixed in place. As each of them was manoeuvred into position the blue tit hopped around to check it, making fussy and rather unnecessary adjustments. It was while he was doing so that he discovered a major error; an enthusiastic but rather confused assistant had hooked an oar through its hole from the top downwards instead of from the bottom upwards. If they had attempted to take off with this mistake undetected Creakwing's weight would have caused the oar to part immediately from the handkerchief and spill him out. The blue tit was clearly delighted by the discovery.

"See that," he cried triumphantly, pointing to the offending oar. "Do I have to do everything?"

For his part Creakwing remained serenely untroubled by this narrow escape. He lay in the centre of the skyboat, smiling amiably in a way that made all the swallows feel distinctly uneasy and spoke only once. His remark was addressed to Bony, rather surprisingly since the old leader had often given the impression that he did not have a very high opinion of his qualities. Bony who never tired of hearing the story of his leader's courageous exploit on that Crossing long ago had now become touchingly concerned for his welfare as the time drew near for them to depart on the same journey. There was a moment when Bony was re-arranging their little store of oars more comfortably around him when Creakwing looked up at him with that strange smile.

"Good evening, my young friend," he said jovially. "I perceive from the cold that we have arrived in the north just a little early. But don't worry. It is spring and it will get much warmer soon, I do assure you."

All the time the busy scene had been growing imperceptibly stiller and quieter as each little task was completed and then at last no matter how hard they looked the swallows could see nothing more to do. They moved to their oars and from his position at the back on the right-hand side Wake surveyed the scene for the last time. It was dusk and the snow had finally come, falling softly into the forest clearing and marking its boundaries with a faint glimmer of light which was growing stronger all the time. This had been a place of mystery ever since his first visit but it had never looked as strange as it did now, amid the whirling and the settling of the snow. Through the gloom he could see the jackdaws clustered in the bare branches of the tree growing out of the ruins. Among them he could just make out the lady jackdaw, she who had made it all possible, but it was too dark to see her eyes. Below him on the ground the blue tit was fussing about, pretending to do something to the folds of the handkerchief while the owl who loved all forms of ceremony had assumed his most imposing manner, the one which tended to suggest that he was about to be marched past.

Wake had often thought about this moment and about how he would conduct himself when it finally came. He had expected to feel solemn and serious, perhaps even to say a few words, but instead he felt only a great impatience to be gone. With the snow falling ever more heavily it was as though winter was making one final, desperate attempt to detain them. All around the skyboat his companions, their tiny bodies already wet with snow, anxiously awaited his signal. There was no time for speeches; they had almost been too late.

"Thank you all for everything you have done," he said. "We will see you in the spring when the swallows return."

And with those words the skyboat rose up into the whirling darkness. For a moment it faltered as the swallows seemed to forget their hard-won skills. The little craft lurched to one side. From the ruins a jackdaw cried out. And then they had recovered and were climbing higher, six sets of wings beating together with growing confidence.

Because of the snow the skyboat was quickly lost to sight but even when it had gone the blue tit remained there, staring up into the night at the playfully billowing snowflakes which had taken the place of the swallows and now, it seemed, were trying to cheer him up....

High above the trees Wake murmured a command and the skyboat banked slightly to the left. Employing the special bounding flight they would use throughout the Crossing, the swallows began to increase their speed, flying so smoothly now that deep in his folds of silk Creakwing did not stir. It was as they were approaching the estuary that Wake began to feel the first stirrings of a familiar apprehension. All that he had learned about the Crossing had convinced him that the stars were important. For that reason he had decided to study them the moment their journey began, just to see if anything occurred to him. Now, though, the stars were veiled by the snow. As he strained to see ahead through the swirling flakes the darkness of the ground below was all at once relieved by the lighter gleam of water. It was the estuary. From his position on the front right-hand oar Bony saw it, too, and looked back, grinning with pleasure. Wake nodded to acknowledge this minor triumph; at least they would not become lost before they had even crossed the estuary! It was at that moment that Bony cried out.

"Up ahead. What are they doing here?"

Wake craned his head to see beyond Bony. There, directly ahead of them, wheeling about in the rapidly darkening sky above the estuary, appearing and disappearing as the light flashed on their wings, were uncountable numbers of gulls, more gulls than he could ever have believed existed, filling the night and blocking the path they must take out across the water. The speed of the skyboat slackened imperceptibly. He could sense the others waiting for some response from him but he had not the faintest idea what it meant and as he tried to think of something re-assuring to say the skyboat continued on a course which would take them right in amongst these mysterious intruders.

Had the gulls perhaps flown up to say good-bye? This was unlikely; after all it had been agreed that the swallows would leave as discreetly as possible; in any case if this was the explanation why were they making no move to greet the swallows? Something else was puzzling; gulls were notoriously noisy, but despite their vast numbers the birds massing in the sky ahead of them were making not a sound.

It was when they reached the shore of the estuary that the swallows learned the truth. The gulls had gone there not to say good-bye but to help. There was nothing random about their movements, as had at first appeared; they were in fact flying out across the estuary to the other side and back again, backwards and forwards, repeatedly, in two endless lanes, to form a living pathway stretching out before them through the confusion of the snow and the night, all the way to the distant shore, and all they had to do to cross in safety was to pass between them.

And that was how the swallows left their summer home behind at last, to begin their perilous journey to the south, venturing out from land for the very first time on that cold winter night down a glimmering avenue of birds from whom there came not a sound but the rush of their wings, mingling with the rush of the wind, so that not another living creature looked up to see them go.

* * *

Chapter 15

In future years whenever a group of young swallows found themselves roosting with older birds and the conversation turned as it often did to the tale of the Winter Crossing the hardest thing for many of them to accept was the idea of winter itself. The reason why water went hard; the function of trees with no leaves; the explanation for clouds descending from the sky to go drifting across the land; the purpose of the east wind; and the theory and practice of snow.

I will be frank; many young swallows never fully learned to accept these amazing ideas. Whenever they were mentioned they would look at each other in a knowing sort of way or cast their eyes upwards in dramatic scorn; sometimes they would even snort in a manner bordering on the offensive and say: "A likely story. You must think we were born yesterday." (The fact that in most cases this was almost literally true did not seem to occur to them.)

There was one feature of the story which truly astonished them. It concerned something which was said to have happened soon after the great journey had begun, as the swallows prepared to adjust their course for the first time. Although Wake was still exceedingly vague about how the swallows employed the stars to find their way, other principles of navigation had proved rather easier to understand and he was about to use one now. The swallows had a long-established navigational aid which became especially important when the visibility was poor. Living on an enormous long island meant there was always the possibility of drifting off-course and out to sea. To avoid this danger it had become their practice to use the lights of towns and cities to guide them on the journey south. So long as these lights kept appearing they knew they were still on course. They had gone only a short distance beyond the far shore of the estuary when Wake saw what he was looking for. Dimly through the falling snow, below and to their left, the lights of a village had appeared. It was the first of their guidance "beacons". But there was also something else and it was Oliver on the other front oar who saw it first.

"Down there. Right in the middle of the lights. Look!"

Instinctively, all the swallows craned their heads to see. The oars jerked sideways. For a moment the skyboat faltered as they lost the rhythm they had so carefully created. Then Wake's warning cry, urgent with anger, steadied them. Oliver looked anxiously at his leader in a slightly abashed way but was too excited to remain silent. "One of the trees down there is shining."

It was true. Far below them, right in the centre of the little village, dimming the fainter lights around it, there was a shining tree. It was shining with coloured light of every imaginable hue; orange and yellow, green and blue, pink and red. And most wondrous of all, for they had not even known such colours existed, there was gold and silver light.

Ever since the end of summer the swallows had watched their world decaying all around them. At times it had seemed as though every living thing was dying. Nowhere had this been more apparent than in the forest, with winter like a sickness draining all the life from the trees. But now, down below, they could see this wonderful tree, garlanded again in all the bright and lovely colours of summer. It was not hard to believe that it was there to remind them what summer was like and how it would be again. And as that warm and friendly light faded away into the darkness behind them the swallows were strangely uplifted. They were to see many more trees like that in the days which followed, always at the very centre of those clusters of lights guiding them south.

One other strange happening was to puzzle all those young swallows when they learned the story of the Crossing in the years to come. As they hurried across the sky on that very first night Wake and his companions began to hear the sound of bells; it seemed as though the bells were calling to each other in great excitement across the wastes of snow and as the sound rose up and crashed around them in the darkness the swallows were forced to the conclusion that this also was a message intended just for them and were again encouraged. [20]

To avoid attracting attention the swallows had decided to travel

---

[20] *Perhaps I should now make it clear, for the benefit of those among you who always require proof of wonderful things, that some of the more unusual aspects of this story are supported by what are called "affidavits" with very important signatures at the bottom. One of these documents, signed by the Clerk to the council in a certain English parish, confirms the account of shining trees and calling bells and although written in August concludes by wishing me, and no doubt you, all the best for Christmas! Make of that what you will*

only at night. Any worries Wake might have had about navigating in these conditions were quickly dispelled on that very first night as the skies began to clear of snow leaving the landscape below bathed in a glimmering white light which led them steadily south. The clearing skies also revealed the stars in all their complicated splendour but he decided for the time being to ignore them.

As dawn brought an end to the first stage of their journey Wake began looking for a suitable place for the swallows to hide; a place of safety where they could catch a few hours sleep, during those few hours of winter daylight. But even though the sky was growing lighter all the time he was forced to reject several possible places because they were just too busy; the ground below seemed to be crowded with humans trying to cope with the crisis of the weather. For the swallows it was fascinating to observe how awkward and helpless the humans had become with the first snow of the winter but still they could not afford to take the chance of being discovered and Wake was just starting to become quite anxious when he saw the perfect place. It was a farm very much like the one they had just left. After the night of snow it was standing isolated in the middle of a vast and glittering plain of white and emanating a definite air of surprise. As they cautiously descended Wake was re-assured to see no sign of human activity.

He chose the stables. They lay some distance away from the farmhouse itself and, he was pleased to see, were cut off from it by a wide expanse of untrodden snow. Swiftly the swallows flitted inside and alighted with their burden on top of some bales of hay reaching almost to the roof in the gloom at the back of one of the stalls. It was the first time the skyboat had come to rest since leaving the estuary the night before but Creakwing showed no reaction. When they peered inside to see how he had coped with the journey he was still lying fast asleep in the folds of the handkerchief. Even when Bess removed a few of the spare oars which had rolled beneath him he did not stir. As they looked around adjusting to their new surroundings Oliver pointed up above them with a bleak little smile and said: "I see we are not the first." Underneath one of the roof beams they saw a swallows' nest and even though it was hard for them to imagine what this place had been like in summer it was strangely comforting to reflect that swallows just like them had lived there once. Outside, the old building shook and rattled in the icy wind but inside, in the silence, which was deep and old, the swallows felt warm and safe. They were almost asleep when the female blackbird appeared on the sill of the divided door at the entrance to the stable and addressed them.

"Welcome," she said without surprise, as though the little party of swallows had been long expected. "Is there anything we can do to help?"

The swallows exchanged uneasy glances. "How did you know we were here?" said Wake abruptly. He was aware that his response must have sounded distinctly unfriendly but this blackbird's cheerful greeting had seemed to mock all his attempts to keep their movements secret. His eyes scanned the patch of sky behind the visitor for more surprises. But the blackbird seemed not at all disconcerted by his response. She surveyed the little group of swallows in a friendly sort of way.

"Many birds are looking out for you," she said, "but I had no idea you would pass this way."

Wake was just pondering the disturbing possibility that vast numbers of hidden eyes had been following their progress south when the female blackbird was joined on top of the door by two younger birds. They were clearly her offspring. First they edged as close to their mother as possible and then they began to examine the swallows with expressions in which awe and nervousness seemed equally mixed.

The blackbird regarded them with amusement for a moment and then she turned her gaze on Wake again and said: "You are Wake, the swallow. You and your friends are already very famous. And if there is anything we can do...." As her voice trailed away, he saw that the lady blackbird's eyes were also honouring him and felt an old discomfort.

"No, there is nothing we need, thank you," he said. "Except a little time for sleep. We have been travelling all night and we must be on our way again in a few hours. It would be helpful if we could all rest together, without the need to keep watch."

The blackbird looked excessively gratified. "The blackbirds will watch over you. It will be an honour to see that you are not disturbed." She cleared her throat in an alarmingly familiar way. "If there is any danger we will sing."

For the few short hours of daylight still remaining the lady blackbird and her young ones watched over the swallows but to her regret there was no cause for alarm and therefore no occasion for her to sing.

In the days which followed there were to be many such encounters. Not once did the swallows descend towards a new resting place after a night of flying without being observed and greeted. Resident birds of every conceivable species had mysteriously heard of their coming and longed to be involved in some way. On several occasions they were shown into barns or sheds where swallows had lived in the summer and whenever this happened it seemed to the travellers that the memory of the birds which had lived there was also protecting and sustaining them as they journeyed south.

Early one morning the swallows took refuge in a shed in a cottage garden. The snow was floating down in thick, wet lumps. All the humans were sheltering indoors and they were certain that no one could possibly have noticed their arrival but they were mistaken. Inside the shed they made themselves comfortable on a pile of empty sacks while Wake went to the window for a last check before they settled down.

The concentrated gaze of the starlings fell upon him with the force of a blow. They had arrived without a sound and were now assembled in a long line, just a short distance away, on a telephone wire running across the garden, innumerable birds scrutinising the shed from their sagging perch and waiting with unaccustomed patience to be noticed.

Scarcely daring to remove his gaze for fear of provoking them into movement Wake breathed a warning to the others. Bony appeared beside him in the window. "There are seventeen," he said helpfully. "Nineteen," corrected Oliver nervously, from the other side. Wake decided not to count them in case there were even more.

The swallows were well aware of the tendency of starlings to do everything together but they had not appreciated that on occasions, if they wished to create a bit of an impression, they were perfectly capable of speaking as one. From their communal throat came the perfectly enunciated request to be allowed to help. The sound was so unusual that Wake found himself inquiring what the starlings thought they might do, merely to experience once more that extraordinary sound. Again, that communal beak gaped open and the starlings chorused their willingness to have a look round for some food.

They certainly did their best; indeed they did manage to produce a few modest little oddments which were vaguely reminiscent of food. And the swallows consumed them uneasily, in a strained silence, under the gaze of one wide and enormous starling eye. A few days later, while settling down in a woodshed, in the shadow of a secluded forest, tired and hungry as usual, the swallows were visited by an owl who had thoughtfully prepared a lecture to welcome them, just in case they happened to pass by.

"There is no time like the present," he said, making himself rather worryingly comfortable on a workbench. "Travel broadens the mind, they say, and you will enjoy your stay so much more if you have learned something about the country you are going to, so I will now give you a brief outline of the geography, topography, biography and autobiography of Africa, and afterwards you can ask questions."

At the end of his address no questions occurred to the swallows, mainly because they were fast asleep, and shortly afterwards the owl departed, with the satisfied air of one who has nobly played his part on the stage of history in momentous times.

A strange new elation now gripped the swallows. With every day that passed their confidence grew. Everything was going precisely to plan. The main source of their anxiety had long since disappeared: the skyboat was handling beautifully and they could now fly instinctively without even thinking about it. As each day brought them closer to that long-awaited re-union they found themselves trying to imagine how the main community of swallows would react when the skyboat appeared at last in the northern sky. They began to think more about their parents; to remember how pleasant it had been to be worried about and how nice it would be to be a source of anxiety once more.

Strange, then, to reflect that in those moments of increasing joy and confidence the swallows were about to be plunged into the most terrible danger because of a mistake on the very first night of their journey; a mistake they did not even know they had made and for which their inexperienced leader was directly responsible.

* * *

129

Chapter 15

On the seventh night after their departure the swallows began to smell the sea. It was a moment they had been expecting. They knew their course should take them out across the sea just once and after that the only ordeal remaining would be the long journey over the desert to their winter home. Only one thing puzzled Wake; they had reached the sea a great deal sooner than he expected!

The skyboat flew on through the numbing cold of the winter night with that salty odour growing stronger all the time. The patches of light where towns and villages lay below grew fewer and then there was only the dark. With those comforting beacons gone the swallows felt a growing sense of isolation and then just before dawn they heard the sound of waves crashing unseen on the rocks below and the wind began to sing. Bony turned and grinned, and then the swallows were passing out over the sea.

Steadily, the skyboat moved on through the night with the sea prowling about in the darkness far below. From his discussions with Creakwing Wake knew that if all went well this stage should take all the following day but the fact that they would be flying in daylight for the first time did not trouble him, since there would be no one there to observe them, out above the empty sea.

At dawn, for the first time, they saw the sea and the sight of it silenced them all. It was everywhere; a wilderness of water tossing and tumbling wherever they looked and even though they knew they were still far from land the swallows began peering straight ahead, through flurries of sleety snow, merely to divert their gaze from the awful sight below.

By midday there was still no sign of land and at the front of the skyboat Bony and Oliver were turning round to look at him with growing frequency. They had been in continuous flight since the late afternoon of the previous day, longer than ever before, and for the first time Wake began to consider the possibility that something had gone wrong. He recalled Creakwing once saying that strong head-winds could often slow the swallows down, prolonging the sea crossing. There was only one problem with this explanation-- they were experiencing tail-winds; the wind was actually assisting them rather than slowing them down. So where was the land?

With the wind growing stronger all the time the handkerchief had become a billowing sail and they had to fight to control it.

Bony and Oliver at the front no longer turned round to consult him; their eyes remained studiously fixed on the empty prospect in front of them. Even Harold on the opposite oar carefully avoided his eyes by peering elaborately ahead. Only Bess and Winnie on the two central oars gave the impression of being wonderfully unperturbed. Their anxiety appeared to be reserved for Creakwing. The turbulence was tossing him about, from one side of the skyboat to the other, and although his eyes remained tightly closed occasionally he would groan faintly. Because of their central position it had become their responsibility to try to ensure that the fold in the middle of the handkerchief remained deep enough to prevent him falling out.

All through the afternoon the swallows flew on. The sea now seemed much closer. Sometimes when two great waves crashed together they actually felt the spray reaching up for them. By late afternoon it was clear that they were tiring; the pace of the skyboat had imperceptibly slackened. Wake did not order it; it was as though they had all decided at the same time that it was madness to continue to race across the sky when there was no indication of land ahead, only the endless emptiness of the prowling sea.

Throughout the afternoon the flurries of sleet and snow had been dying out and now at dusk they ceased altogether and the clouds began to clear. For the first time that day the sun shone through, straight ahead and so low in the sky that it dazzled them. It was as he narrowed his eyes against that blinding light that Wake finally remembered; he remembered a conversation with Creakwing; a casual remark, during one of those long summer afternoons, about the way the swallows used the sun to guide them during the Crossing. If you were flying south, he had said, you kept the sun on your left in the morning and in the evening on your right. If you were flying north it was the other way round. It was now evening and the sun was not on either side; it was straight ahead and blinding him with its brilliance. They were wildly off-course.

"Turn left--now," he screamed. "We're going the wrong way!"

The swallows turned in the sky with a savage elation, wrenching the little craft round so violently that they almost lost control. At last they were doing something positive. Now the dying sun was on their right, exactly as Creakwing had indicated. And as though encouraged by this decisive action the skyboat began to pick up speed again.

Wake was consumed by shame. He who was supposed to be their leader had forgotten this elementary principle of navigation. As to how the mistake had occurred in the first place, that was still a complete mystery; they had travelled south carefully following the lights until they reached the coast and he had not the faintest idea what could have gone wrong to lead them out across the open sea in entirely the wrong direction. And that troubled him even more. His only consolation was the knowledge that he had now corrected his error. Unable to confide in the others about how near they had come to disaster, he found himself fervently hoping that he had not left it too late.

Soon afterwards the sun fell below the horizon and darkness descended once more over the monotonous waves. The swallows did not know it but they were now adding another awesome detail to the legend of the Winter Crossing; never before in recorded memory had swallows remained in continuous flight over the sea for so long. All through the night they flew on, close to exhaustion, with the wind growing stronger all the time. Since they had adjusted their course it was no longer a tailwind; now it was buffeting them from the side and remorselessly slowing them down. At the same time the wind was rousing the sea. They could hear the waves below, roaming about in the darkness and crashing blindly together with a great roar, tossing towering fountains of foam high in the air towards them. Sometimes the cascading spray would actually drench the skyboat and when this happened Creakwing would stir uneasily in the depths of the handkerchief.

As the light grew stronger on that second morning over the sea nothing was said but the swallows were confident that this time they would see the land, preferably close at hand but acceptable even on the far horizon. Since they were not at all certain, after all the confusion, in which direction it might lie they scanned the horizon in a broad sweep from left to right. The land was not there. Instead an appalling sight met their eyes; a sight so unexpected that all Wake's hard-won powers of leadership deserted him and he could only gaze around him like the others, transfixed with fear.

Unnoticed in the night, the skyboat had lost so much height that it appeared to be flying below the sea. Great flowing plains of foaming water ran away in all directions, rising steeply, here and there, up glassy slopes, sheer and streaming, to towering crests where the howling wind was tearing off flakes of foam and hurling them wildly into the mist of rain and spray far above them. The sky had gone and everywhere was water. But miraculously, for at times they were actually looking *up* at the sea, they were still unscathed. Desperately the swallows fought to regain height; to escape from that watery abyss. And as the skyboat slowly rose from the streaming and gurgling gloom between the waves, and up towards the brightening morning light, Bess cried out in wonder.

"There are birds. There are birds down below. On the water."

At first the others could see nothing and thought she must be mistaken and then away to their right a wave rolled past and there they were. There were five or six of them, birds of a kind they had never seen before, actually resting on the surface of the water and moving to the motion of the waves. As the swallows watched, the mysterious birds were borne up the side of a wave to the very crest and then as it bloomed with foaming spray they rose lazily into the air to settle down once more in the calm on the other side. It was utterly astonishing to see them there, amid all that turbulent commotion, riding up the waves and down again as serenely as the ducks on the pond back home.

Wake was nervously pondering the advisability of trying to attract their attention, although not at all clear how these strange birds might help them, when the decision was taken for him. One of them looked up and spotted the swallows and a moment later they had risen from the waves and were flying up towards the skyboat.

The swallows watched in silence as the newcomers positioned themselves alongside the skyboat, beaming nervously since it was now apparent that these mysterious birds were much larger and stronger than they had seemed from above. For a few moments none of the six birds made any move to communicate with the swallows. Instead they concentrated on positioning themselves very precisely alongside the fluttering handkerchief, clearly anxious to avoid becoming entangled in it. If they were puzzled or intrigued by the swallows and their skyboat they gave not the slightest sign. Finally they appeared to be satisfied with both their bearing and their speed and the one who was obviously their leader turned his head towards the apprehensive swallows.

"Petrel patrol at your service," he said, to no one in particular, with just a hint of amusement. "You seem to be in some difficulty. May I request that you follow us?"

In years to come, whenever he reflected upon the events of the

Crossing, Wake was never really able to think of the petrels as being birds in the sense that the swallows were. For two days and two nights the terrors of the sea had occupied all their thoughts. The reality of this experience had been far worse than they had ever imagined. And yet here were birds which actually lived out there upon the waves, apparently unperturbed by the chaos and the danger of the sea. Their upbringing had clearly been quite different from that of the swallows. Were they the birds mentioned by the gull on that last evening before the swallows left the estuary? He did not know. In any case, what did it matter? The swallows were completely lost and exhausted and if at that moment the land was quite near, hidden just beyond these towering seas, these mysterious strangers were the only ones capable of showing them the way.

"We do seem to be a little lost," he said. "We would be grateful if you would guide us towards the land."

Only Bony at the front seemed a little churlish about the situation, as though mildly offended by the notion that he might need assistance.

"We were heading for Africa," he told the nearest petrel. "I dare say we would have found it eventually."

"Found the South Pole more likely, matey," replied the petrel amiably.

Although the petrels showed no real inclination to talk it was quite clear that they were fascinated by the concept of the skyboat and the techniques involved in flying it, so for the next few minutes, as they flew on, in what they presumed to be the direction of land, the swallows put on a modest flying display, tending, as one does on these occasions, to exaggerate the difficulties in order to demonstrate how skilfully they could cope with them.

But the land was not their destination. They had been flying for about fifteen minutes, following the course indicated to them by the petrels, when there ahead of them, looming out of the spray and the rain, lying right across their path, as substantial as the land itself, the astonished swallows saw for the first time the gigantic shape of an ocean-going ship. The petrel leader seemed quietly satisfied to have located the vessel in such weather, among all those endless ranges of towering and tumbling water.

"It's a freighter," he shouted to the swallows. "Eight days out of Lagos and bound for London. We usually know where they are. Just in case we need them in an emergency. That's where we're headed but I want to come in astern of her and board her on the boat-deck, to avoid being spotted."

Baffled by these nautical references and hoping that the petrel leader had not said anything too important, the swallows concentrated on following his instructions. Gradually the skyboat came closer to the enormous bulk of the freighter. Even approaching astern of her the swallows found themselves awed by the proportions of the vessel they had come upon so unexpectedly, lying out there in the middle of the ocean. From time to time, as the wind tossed the little craft across the sky, the petrel leader called out adjustments to their course, until at last they found themselves in the lee of the wind, sheltered by the high stern of the vessel. The noise of the past two days and nights abated and in the sudden calm the swallows could hear only the hiss of the water down the long sides of the ship and the deep, hidden pounding of the propellers.

"A little way for'ard. Do you see it? The boat deck. Now wait for my signal."

The skyboat was now so close to the great vessel that the sheer iron walls of its enormous stern, black and stained with rust, towered above them from just a few yards away. Their speeds were now exactly matched and so the distance between the swallows and the ship remained constant. A few tense moments passed in this way, as they awaited the signal from the petrel leader. Then the mighty ship began to settle down into the trough of a wave. Down and down it plunged. Wake watched in fascination, convinced that it must finally plunge beneath the waves. The boat deck came rushing down towards them and a moment later they were actually looking down on the deck of the ship. Exposed once more to the full fury of the storm they would probably have been borne backwards if the escorting birds had not seen the danger. The two petrels flying alongside Bony and Oliver closed in swiftly and gripped the two front oars to steady them.

"Go!" screamed the petrel leader. "Make for the lifeboat."

Assisted by the two petrels at the front the swallows quickly descended towards a double row of lifeboats in the stern of the ship. Canvas sheets tied down with rope protected them from the weather, apart from the one nearest to the stern rails which showed a small gap where its cover had been rolled back.

"In there."

Wake wondered if it was going to be possible in that wind to manoeuvre the skyboat and its oars through that narrow opening but he had under-estimated their own remarkable skills; and the strength of their two helpers. The skyboat passed through the gap without difficulty and into the lifeboat. Only the petrel leader entered with them; the others soared high above the lifeboat, balanced for a moment on the wind to grin their farewells, and were then borne backwards and away.

Coming in to land Wake had noticed that the lifeboats were suspended from stanchions high above the deck, quite inaccessible to anyone who might walk past; he had also noticed that the deck itself was quite deserted, plunging and rearing and awash with foaming water as the great ship struggled against the fury of the storm. They were safe from discovery. For the first time in two days and two nights the swallows relaxed their grip on the oars and sank down exhausted, eyes closed, relishing the silence and the stillness in which the only sound came from the canvas cover fluttering in the wind just above their heads.

"It's not much I'm afraid, shipmates," observed the petrel leader loudly, as though he was still outside and straining to be heard above the noise of the wind.

Wearily the swallows opened their eyes to look around them. The petrel had been unduly modest. They were lying on a soft bed made up of odd scraps of material, strewn out along the bottom of the boat beneath the seats, to form a sort of elongated nest.

"I don't rightly know if it's anything like a swallows' nest since I've never clapped eyes on one myself but it's the best we can do. We try to keep one boat ready in case of emergencies but we never know what kind of birds are going to drop in."

So this strange ocean bird who seemed so much at ease out here among the waves, far from land, knew that they were swallows. From his bed at the bottom of the boat Wake discreetly studied their rescuer as he perched above them on one of the lifeboat seats. Apart from the pale bars on his wings and tail his feathers were entirely black. His beak was long and curved with a sort of bump in the middle which gave him a foreign and oddly villainous appearance. He was large and powerfully built. And he smelled of the sea. The petrel would have been altogether a most disturbing presence at such close quarters if the gaze of those dark eyes had not been steady and warm.

The petrel continued to survey the swallows from his vantage point above, swaying easily to the movement of the ship, as it pitched and rolled in the heavy seas, and then he said: "I think I know who you are."

Even Wake who was by now accustomed to their apparently universal fame was a little surprised to be unmasked out there on the ocean waves.

"Yes," mused the petrel, "I was having a chat with a tern[21] a couple of weeks ago. He was on his way south and had to heave-to behind the boat for a few hours, to ride out a storm. He told me a very strange yarn." The petrel paused, awaiting their full attention. "I think you must be the winter swallows."

"That's us," confirmed Bony, before any of the others could speak.

"Adrift," said the petrel, "and heading nowhere in particular."

"Actually we were heading south," corrected Bony. "To Africa."

"West, Sou'west, matey. Humbly begging your pardon; away from Africa. It's a very big place, I grant you, but you'd have missed it easily."

The petrel beamed down at the swallows, as though perfectly prepared to impart more of this nautical information if required.

"Don't you ever get lost yourselves?" inquired Bess politely. "The sea seems to be an awfully big place."

"I dare say we do from time to time," said the petrel, "but when everywhere looks the same it's hard to tell really."

Winnie gave a little shiver of distaste. "Do you actually live out here all the time?"

"Out where?"

"Out in the middle of the sea."

"That," said the petrel, "depends on your point of view. The way we look at it you swallows live out there." And here the petrel pointed vaguely to the north.

"Don't you get bored living in the middle of the sea?" said Harold.

"Let me ask you a question," said the petrel. "Does the land move about beneath you?"

---

[21] *Most migrant birds would probably agree that the Arctic tern is the champion of them all. He regularly travels up and down the world between the Arctic and the Antarctic and for this reason he is much appreciated as a source of news and gossip for birds like the petrel which sometimes hardly see a soul to talk to for months on end.*

Harold shook his head.

"Is it different every day?"

"No."

"Does it sing to you at night?"

Harold looked thoroughly baffled and shook his head again.

"Of course not," protested Winnie, coming to his rescue.

"Well, I can quite see how you would find the sea boring after all that excitement," murmured the petrel.

"Don't you ever visit the land?" inquired Bess.

"Just once a year, in the spring. But to tell you the truth we always leave as soon as we can. The land's far too flat for us and we don't like the way it never moves."

"Why?" enquired Bony".

"Why what?"

"Why do you visit the land once a year?"

The petrel gazed down at Bony in a thoughtful sort of way, as though pondering the possibility that the question had some deeper, hidden meaning, while the two females regarded him pityingly.

"Why do you think?" said Winnie archly, and Bess blushed.

Soothed by these solemn inanities and lulled by the sound of the canvas cover gently flapping in the wind just above his head, utterly at peace in the deep folds of the warm bed in the bottom of the boat, Wake was actually falling asleep when the petrel's voice and manner abruptly changed.

"No more questions for now, shipmates. We can talk later. Time for you to sling your hammocks and turn in. You've come a long way already but there's a long way still to go and you have to be on your way again as soon as you've rested." He hopped to the opening in the canvas cover and was about to disappear when Wake remembered something.

"Excuse me, sir."

"Skipper," said the petrel. "Not 'sir'. It's just one of those nautical traditions; as head of the search and rescue service for this sector I'm known as 'skipper'."

"Er, skipper," said Wake, in an experimental sort of way, "I just wanted to suggest that as we are all quite tired from the journey and you've been kind enough to make us very comfortable we might rest here for a few days before setting off again."

"Well, ordinarily that might have been quite a good idea," agreed the petrel. "You wouldn't be the first migrants to be blown off course and take refuge on a ship. But I'm afraid that won't be possible this time. I wasn't going to tell you until you'd rested but I'm afraid we've hit a little snag." He looked down at the swallows with a concealing smile. "It's nothing to worry about but I'm afraid this boat isn't actually going your way. In fact, it's taking you back to where you came from."

* * *

Chapter 16

Utterly exhausted, safe at last from the fury of the sea and enveloped in the folds of the makeshift bed at the bottom of the lifeboat, the swallows drifted slowly into sleep but for Wake it was a sleep haunted by dreams of winter....

He was the last swallow in the world. For some unaccountable reason he had forgotten how to fly and so he hopped across the frozen fields. Flurries of snow and blossom all blew together, as he made his way towards the forest. Inside among the trees, although there was not a breath of wind, the bare branches were all moving, bending their cold limbs down towards the earth and tenderly caressing their own lost leaves scattered on the ground. Right in the middle of the forest he found himself standing under a shining tree. On a branch just above him two magpies cackled with helpless laughter. Sitting alongside them in the tree and trying not to smile, was his old friend the duck. And on the topmost branch, among the coloured blooms of light, the little yellow bird sat pointing imploringly to the south.....

For hour after hour the swallows slept on in their snug little haven. They were too exhausted to care that they were now being carried back in the direction they had come from, back to the winter. As they slept on, the storm began at last to abate and as night fell a bank of fog drifted in across the sea from the north. The engines of the great ship ceased to pound and a deep calm settled on the ocean.

Wake was the first to open his eyes. For a few moments he lay there, aware of a new and oppressive silence. For some reason the boat was no longer moving and he could hear voices. Whoever it was they were speaking softly as though anxious not to disturb the sleeping swallows. Then he recognised them. One was the leader of the petrels who must have returned while they were sleeping and the other... Wake's eyes opened and he stared up in astonishment from the bottom of the boat. The other was Creakwing, perched alongside the petrel on one of the lifeboat seats and looking down at him with every indication that everything was quite normal and exactly as expected.

"Ah, you are awake," he whispered. "Come and join us. We were just discussing the situation."

Wake had no idea how long he had been asleep but it was clear that during that time Creakwing had somehow recovered from his fever and was now engaged in serious discussions with the petrel about what was to be done. Proud anger swept through him at the thought. This was his plan they were talking about. How dare Creakwing sit there calmly discussing what was to happen next when he had been unconscious and helpless up to a very short time ago? So great was his indignation at the thought of it that there is no knowing what he would have said, if at that very moment the noise had not begun.

It was far and away the worst noise he had ever heard; so deep and loud and long that even when it had stopped it was possible to think it was still going on. Judging by their reaction it probably ranked very highly as a noise so far as his companions were concerned. In a dazed panic, with escape their only thought, the swallows dived for the oars of the skyboat; all except Bony. Devoid of oars, he rose sharply upwards, in a highly personalised way, only to find his ardent ascent swiftly concluded, in a substantial crash and a howl of pain, as he struck the canvas just above his head. It was the petrel leader, looking down in some amusement from his vantage point above the swallows who quelled the panic.

"It was a fog warning. It'll go again in a minute. Nothing to worry about."

The sight of Creakwing sitting there above them, apparently fully recovered and exuding all his old authority, was totally unexpected. No one seemed to know what to say so Bess broke the silence by inquiring after his health.

"A little weak still," he replied, "but getting stronger all the time."

There was an awkward pause. One or two of the swallows glanced at Wake and he could sense the question in their eyes. With Creakwing apparently recovered who was now in charge? Who was their leader? He still felt resentful about the fact that he had woken from sleep to hear the two older birds discussing his plan. On the other hand, what possible justification could he have for continuing to assert his authority over the swallows? Because of his inexperience they had taken the wrong course, been rescued from almost certain death by the petrels and were now lying lost and exhausted on a ship which was taking them back where they had come from. So, they wondered, who was their leader? Was it the swallow who was responsible for their present plight or had he yielded his authority to Creakwing, the wise and experienced veteran of many such crossings?

"We were just discussing what went wrong," said Creakwing. He smiled sympathetically. "It was probably the wind."

The petrel nodded his agreement. "The wind can change tack completely in these northern latitudes in winter; strong easterlies; they can blow you right off course."

"You'd have been better making allowances for the wind," said Creakwing.

"Trimming sail and altering course a few points to the south," said the petrel.

Carefully, Wake explained how they had followed the lights, from the first night, all the way down to the coast.

"That doesn't mean anything," said Creakwing. "There would be lights even if all the time you were being blown off-course. I reckon you must have crossed the coast to the west instead of the south." He regarded Wake steadily for a moment and said: "Why didn't you navigate by the stars?"

Wake felt the others looking at him. The same question was in their faces. If you're a leader why didn't you use the stars? That is what leaders do. Only Bess spoke up for him.

"It was cloudy and snowing for most of the time. We couldn't even see the stars."

Wake knew that this was not the whole truth and he knew that Creakwing was aware of it, too. There had been clear interludes when the stars were in view, several of them. The reason he had not utilised them was for the old reason; he had not the faintest idea what was supposed to happen when he did. And no one, it seemed, was prepared to tell him. The result was that he felt neither fully confident in the role of leader nor completely comfortable in the role of a swallow content to follow others. Not for the first time he felt miserable and isolated by his failure to comprehend this great mystery.

The old leader seemed to sense his uncertainty.

"Listen to me, boy." Their glances met and it was as though they were alone, back home again in the north, sitting in the sunshine around the barn with everywhere hot and still as far as the eye could see and the awful sea far away and Creakwing talking to him about the role of the leader. "I cannot fly. The fever's gone but I can't fly. I've tried to use the wing while you were asleep but it's hopeless.

What it needs is a bit of sunshine on it and that's not likely to happen out here. If we are going to get off this ship and home to Africa we are going to have to use that contraption of yours and you are going to have to lead. I'll help you all I can but I can't take over now; not after being asleep for most of the Crossing. Whatever you may think, you are probably the only one who knows where we are." He studied the young swallow carefully for a moment. "But you won't do it unless you use all your powers."

So, Wake reflected, Creakwing still believed in him, at least for the time being. He felt a little of his lost pride returning. "If the ship is going the wrong way," he said, "don't you think we should get off it now?"

"No point in doing that, matey," said the petrel. "Not in this fog but don't worry. She's only making a few knots; skipper doesn't want to risk a collision in this lot."

"The petrel has a plan," said Creakwing. "So, with your permission, I'd like to ask him to explain."

The petrel looked down at the swallows. First he glared with enormous ferocity and then he grinned in a most confusing manner.

"Before I tell you the plan I want to say a word about this whole ridiculous business. Whether you like it or not, shipmates, you and your skyboat are now famous. There probably aren't many birds in the northern hemisphere which haven't heard of you and I wouldn't be surprised if the birds in Africa know you are coming. That means that the petrels are going to be talked about, too, so I don't want anything to go wrong. We have a reputation to think of."

Once more the petrel glared and grinned in rapid succession. "What I propose is possibly a little dangerous but it should work, if you all do as you are told. It has to work because it's now your only chance. You have to get off this boat and there is no telling when the fog will lift.

"Now I'm going outside with your leader here." As the petrel's glance singled him out Wake looked up at Creakwing and the old leader smiled and nodded in a solemn sort of way.

"I want the rest of you to stay inside, out of sight. Seven swallows all together in the middle of winter is a bit much to swallow (pardon the pun)-- particularly as the ship happens to be travelling north-- and I don't want to attract the attention of the crew." He glanced down at the skyboat, shook his head in exaggerated disbelief and added: "I'm going to have to borrow that thing, too."

At that moment all further speech and even thought became impossible for the swallows, as the great ship, like a blinded beast, moaned again, long and piteously just above their heads. And that was also the moment when Wake began to have the strangest, secret feeling that he and he alone could actually see up through the drifting fog to the clear skies beyond where the stars were waiting.

Outside the lifeboat it was dark but everywhere was clearly illuminated because the great ship had all its lights on as it edged slowly forward through the fog. The lights were even bright enough to reveal the dark waves lolling peacefully all around the ship as though resting from their exertions during the storm. Because of the brightly shining lights the night had an eventful air, as though something was about to happen, but for as far as Wake could see the deck of the ship stretched away, deserted and silent.

The air was cold and clammy, making him shiver and he could not think why the petrel had brought him outside on such a night. He appreciated the need to leave the ship as quickly as possible but surely they could have waited until daybreak before taking any action. Even though the ship was heading back the way they had come it was moving only very slowly through the fog.

The petrel leader nudged him and pointed at the ship's rails and he saw that the other petrels had now returned and were perched in a line just below the lifeboats. For some reason they exuded an air of secret excitement.

"Right," said the petrel leader. "Do you agree that the basic problem is how to get away from this ship when you can't see where you're going because of the fog?" Wake nodded. "All right, now I want you to watch what happens very carefully," and he gave a little signal to the bird at the front of the line. The petrel turned to the others, grinned expectantly and rose into the air.

At first it flew straight and level, right down the middle of the ship, with Wake straining to follow its outline in the drifting fog. Then it began to rise sharply as it approached an enormous funnel which was easy to distinguish since it was painted bright red. Keeping his eyes fixed firmly on the petrel and wondering what was going to happen he was surprised to see it pass directly over the top of the funnel --and vanish.

He turned to the petrel leader with the intention of making some tactful inquiry about this sad conclusion to the demonstration, only to see that he was quite unperturbed by the disappearance.

"Next."

This time, to concentrate on the fate of the second petrel, he screwed up his eyes even more dramatically. The same thing happened. He was able to watch the progress of the petrel all the way down the ship until the moment when it flew over the top of the funnel. At that point it also vanished. Wake comforted himself with the thought that wherever the petrels might be at least they were probably together.

The petrel leader seemed considerably amused by his perplexity. "This time, as he goes over the funnel keep your eyes on the bit of sky directly above it."

The third petrel took off and for the first time Wake was able to observe precisely what happened. As it reached the point where it was directly above the funnel the petrel suddenly opened its wings and rose up into the swirling darkness, so swiftly that again he almost missed it, and vanished.

"It's a little game we play," said the petrel leader. "To pass the time."

As he spoke the three petrels re-appeared and alighted on the ship's rail. They seemed a little breathless but still elated by the demonstration. The petrel leader acknowledged their assistance with a slight nod and went on: "Don't get me wrong. We love the sea; wouldn't live anywhere else but the time can drag a bit, especially when the waves are rather quiet like they are now. It means you have to create your own amusements. So we play this little game. It's what they call a traditional pastime; petrels learn to do it almost as soon as they can fly.

"Have you ever heard of a thermal?" Wake shook his head. "Lots of birds use them to gain height. Only they use the heat of the sun. Not like us." He pointed away down the ship to where the enormous red funnel was gleaming through the fog. "There's a column of hot air coming out of there all the time--don't ask me why--and if the weather is calm and the ship is going slowly like tonight it goes straight upwards. After a bit of practice you can judge it, so that as soon as you go over the top the hot air wafts you straight up into the sky; higher than a bird can fly. It's a lot of fun, really."

The petrels arranged along the rail grinned and nodded their approval of this sentiment. Just for a moment Wake was appalled by the possibility that the petrel was suggesting this diversion for the swallows while they waited for the fog to lift.

"The interesting thing about it," the petrel continued, "is that on nights like this it's possible to soar straight up through the fog until you come out on the other side where it's perfectly clear." He smiled, as though this was the best part. "And you can see the stars."

"But swallows can't do that," Wake protested. "And we couldn't possibly learn in time."

"You won't have to. In any case you'd probably kill yourselves. Those thermals are very hot where they come out of the funnel. You have to judge it very carefully. Now I want you to watch this." He turned to the petrels on the rail. "This time we'll try it with this contraption."

The petrels grinned in anticipation and moved into position beside the skyboat. Wake saw that they had removed the two central oars, leaving only those at the back and the front. It was strange and just a little worrying to know that birds other than the swallows were now handling the skyboat; not only handling it but making alterations; especially as they apparently now intended to conduct a quite hazardous experiment. If anything went wrong and the skyboat was damaged that would be the end of their journey and probably the end of the swallows, too.

The petrel leader seemed to sense his anxiety. "Don't worry if they don't get it right first time. They've never done anything quite like this before but they are very experienced funnellers."

"Funnellers?"

"That's what we call it --- funnelling."

As it happened the demonstration was surprisingly successful. Operating the oars precisely as they had observed the swallows doing, the four petrels guided the skyboat down the centre of the deck and up through the swirling fog towards the rim of the great funnel. What happened next was even more startling because a slight shimmering of the air was the only indication of the hot gases gushing from the top of it. Precisely over the centre of the funnel, but a safe distance above, in one co-ordinated movement, the petrels opened their wings to receive the full force of that blast of heat. At the same time the silk handkerchief filled like a sail; and they were propelled upwards through the fog with such speed that almost instantly they disappeared from sight. But a moment later they appeared again, away on the port beam and flying low.

"Lost it," observed the petrel leader imperturbably. "Nothing to worry about. Practice makes perfect, as the midshipman said----"

----"when he couldn't stop the ship going around in circles," chorused the petrels still left on the rail, while the petrel leader affected to be greatly astonished by their uncanny ability to know what he would say next.

The jokey manner of the petrels helped to make Wake feel a little less anxious; and so did their determination to master the problem of controlling the skyboat. Time and again they made runs over the funnel; each time they varied their speed and height until eventually every time they returned to their leader it was to report that they had successfully ridden the thermal up through the fog to the other side. Only then did he pronounce himself satisfied.

"And what do the swallows do while the petrels are flying the skyboat?" inquired Wake nervously.

"They hang on," said the petrel, a trifle callously. He turned to his companions. "Did you see the stars?"

"Any amount," said one.

"More than enough," said another.

"Far too many," said a third.

At which they all grinned at the little swallow re-assuringly, as though the sheer quantity of stars in the sky must ensure his success.

Conscious more than ever of the ceaseless pounding of the engines bearing them back slowly but relentlessly in the direction they had come from, Wake hurried below to tell the others of the plan. Creakwing obviously knew all about it and listened without expression. The reaction of the others worried him. He had anticipated that he would have to re-assure them about the ability of the petrels to carry out the manoeuvre he had just witnessed; instead he was conscious only that a dreadful lethargy had now descended upon them. They seemed no longer to care what happened. When he finished speaking they gazed back at him indifferently, their eyes occasionally closing from sheer fatigue.

For the first time since leaving the estuary he saw how their appearance had altered; their plumage of iridescent blue and amber and palest cream, one of the loveliest effects of summer, was matted and dull. Winnie now spent the hours when she was not actually flying grooming her feathers, mechanically, endlessly, so that sometimes he wanted to scream at her to stop. She was doing it now.

Finding water was no longer a problem; it lay in little pools all over the canvas sheeting covering the lifeboats. But food was a different matter. When had they last eaten? It must have been well before they set out across the sea. They were all very thin and if they did not find food soon they would have no more strength to continue. An old memory came into his mind, a memory of the pond in summer, with the reeds swaying and rustling in the warm wind, and the swallows soaring and swooping in the sky above at feeding time.

Could it be his fault that those happy days had ended in this way, with the swallows hungry, exhausted and lost in the middle of the ocean? He was gradually becoming convinced that this must be the case. After all, the plan itself had worked perfectly; the skyboat had flown as they had predicted it would. The failure had been one of navigation and navigation was supposed to be his responsibility; that was what leaders were for. Now that things had gone wrong he was also more aware that his right to lead had never been formally established. He had not been chosen according to ancient custom; prepared for the role and tested by other leaders. The older birds who should have sat in judgement upon him had all gone south long before he assumed command of the swallows. His claims had never been tested. Now he was about to face the greatest test of all; the ordeal of the stars. And he had not the faintest idea what was supposed to happen. What was it Creakwing had told him so long ago?

"I cannot speak of these things to you. If I told you what to expect you might simply imagine--or even pretend--that they had happened and that would be very dangerous. For a true leader there is never any doubt."

Now at last that moment had arrived and these dispirited swallows gave every indication that they had ceased to believe in him. And could he really blame them? His gaze lingered on Bess. How could he ask her to face such unknown perils? It was strange how his concern for the safety of their little band always seemed to centre upon her. Ever since they had found themselves left behind in the north she had been the one he worried about. When he tried to imagine their joyful arrival in their southern home it was her he saw, restored to her family and safe and warm in the sun. If he failed her now she would never reach Africa, nor would she return to the north with her sisters to have her babies in the spring. And he blushed inwardly at that particular prospect.

At that moment Bess raised her head and their eyes met in a glance that just went on and on, in great seriousness, until Bess concluded things with a little smile of recognition which was an ending and a beginning, both at the same time, as you will eventually understand.

"So what are we waiting for?" she told the swallows. "The petrels will now take us up to the stars and then Wake will take us home."

* * *

Chapter 17

"Now remember," said the petrel leader, "the moment we come out of the fog and into clear skies we will leave you. There is nothing more we can do after that. Any questions?"

On top of the canvas sheet covering a cosy, little refuge which had already come to seem like home to the wandering swallows they awaited the signal to begin the briefest and most important flight they would ever make. Their preparations had begun an hour earlier but one unforeseen problem after another had delayed them. At first there was some slightly tense merriment, as no fewer than ten petrels attempted to position themselves down the two sides of the skyboat, with some of them greatly exaggerating the difficulties by pretending to walk into each other and fall over with piteous cries of alarm. Creakwing, seated gravely in the centre of the skyboat and exuding the dignified aloofness of those who are about to be transported, allowed the birds to relieve a little of the tension in this way for a few moments before terminating the confusion with one of his little coughs.

Once order had been restored the first problem became apparent; where precisely were the swallows to "hang on", as the petrel leader had blithely put it, while they waited to resume control of the skyboat? At first they considered positioning themselves half-way along the oars, leaving just enough space to allow clearance for the petrels' wings. But of course there was no knot in the middle of the oars for the swallows to brace themselves against because the blue tit had never envisaged them being used in this way. A brief test flight, just a few yards down the deck, demonstrated that with the petrels manning the oars and the swallows clinging on in the middle, with their wings of necessity closed, they were swung about so violently that they were bound to be dislodged during the actual ascent.

After several experiments it was decided that four of the swallows would position themselves at the corners of the handkerchief with their beaks jammed through the holes where the oars were attached and their feet gripping the material. This meant they would be much more secure when subjected to the enormous forces created by the upward thrust of the skyboat. That still left the problem of the central oars. During flight they would not be used because only four of the petrels were required to lift the skyboat and with the central oars unattended they would have greater freedom of movement. The problem was what to do with Bess and Winnie. At first they considered the possibility of getting them to hang on to the edges of the handkerchief like the swallows at the front and rear but yet another experimental flight demonstrated that this would not work; with the two central oars hanging down and the additional weight of Bess and Winnie the skyboat was unsupported at the sides and sagged down ominously under their weight, threatening to tip Creakwing out.

In the end Wake decided to move the two girls back to the rear oars where he and Harold were stationed; this meant it was a bit crowded at the back but a good deal safer for them. This decision was made to seem even more inspired because in the most perfectly natural way he and Bess found themselves sharing one oar. As you will all no doubt discover there are some circumstances in which it is quite deliciously pleasant to be uncomfortable and so far as Wake was concerned this was one of them. Perhaps it was for Bess, too.

At last they were ready. During their preparations the fog seemed to have grown even denser but down the empty deck the lights still blazed, so that they could clearly see the immense shape of the ship's funnel waiting for them. Wake glanced upwards just in case there was some sign of the stars but there was only the dark and the drifting fog. From his position in the middle of the skyboat Creakwing observed the glance and a private smile passed between them. The leader of the petrels who had positioned himself at the right-hand oar in front of Wake turned and began to speak, then stopped as the fog warning sounded and the long, despairing groan once more filled the night. As the sound died away he resumed.

"Remember. When we reach the funnel, hang on. Hang on tight. And close your eyes if you want to."

And so the skyboat set out on the short journey which would take it up to the stars. At first it wavered a little because the petrels' wings were not beating in rhythm but within seconds they had synchronised their movements and were moving steadily and without haste down the middle of the deck towards the funnel. Halfway down the deck the skyboat began to rise towards that gigantic rim and the powerful forces waiting to seize it. At this point several of the swallows shut their eyes; Bess closed hers by the simple expedient of burying her face in one of Wake's folded wings. The funnel grew larger. Then they were directly over its centre. Wake risked one downward glance into awful depths, dark and deep and shaking in the heat. Hot gases hit his body. There was a gasp from the swallows and Bess's head buried itself deeper. For one terrible moment it seemed as though the petrels had misjudged the height and they would all be consumed in the heat. And then a screech of triumph tore through the night and they were rising upwards on waves of shimmering air. Blindly, silk billowing and fluttering around them, their wings closed and useless, the swallows could only cling on until at last they felt the thermal currents cooling beneath them. The wings of the petrels beat faster. Just for a moment it seemed as though the attempt had failed for the fog still enveloped them. But a moment later the petrel leader screamed in triumph. "We're through. Look below."

With a tremendous effort, clinging to his precarious perch at the back and hampered by Bess who still had her face buried in his chest, Wake craned his head downwards. The silent ocean of the fog now rolled beneath them and all that remained above was a tattered veil trailing across the night. As he watched, the last wisps of cloud tore apart. And the stars burst all around them.

The petrel leader wasted no time. As soon as the skyboat was flying straight and level he turned round to Wake.

"Ready?"

They were higher than swallows had ever flown before. Up there above the clouds the night was quiet and still. Instead of the winds which had buffeted them for so long there was now only a steady surge of freezing air. Because they had not moved since the ascent began the swallows were shivering violently. The conditions were perfect, though, for the skyboat. It was moving forward without a tremor and the transfer proved surprisingly easy.

The first stage took place at the front, rather in the manner of trapeze artists. Carefully timing their movements the petrels released their oars just as the swallows swung across to grasp them, Bony snatching his oar with the air of one reclaiming stolen property. He had clearly not enjoyed abandoning his post to cling helplessly to the corner of the skyboat, especially when his replacement had turned out to be both large and efficient.

Winnie and Bess went next, recovering their trailing oars from the middle of the skyboat with even less difficulty and finally Wake called Harold's name and the youngest of the swallows who had ensured his personal safety since take-off by keeping his eyes tightly closed, resumed position alongside his leader at the back. Once more the swallows were in control. For a moment or two the petrels continued to fly alongside the skyboat, ensuring that all was well until at last their leader seemed satisfied.

"Good luck," he cried and then they were gone, diving down through the clear night sky and plunging into the billowing waves of that silent sea of cloud far below.

Bony and Oliver exchanged grins at the front to indicate their pleasure at finding themselves going somewhere once more and the skyboat began to surge resolutely forward again but just as quickly the speed began to slacken and after a few moments Bony turned round with a baffled air.

"Which way?"

Wake could sense the others looking at him with a similar inquiry, although Creakwing continued to sit in the centre of the skyboat gazing imperturbably ahead and saying nothing. From the great dome of night the stars leaned down towards him. How could all that glittering splendour be anything to do with him? How could there be a path intended just for him in all that wilderness of light?

"Which way?" Bony repeated.

Creakwing who was still gazing calmly ahead from the middle of the skyboat turned and addressed Wake. "In view of all the commotion may I suggest that you fly a little distance away from the skyboat so that you can concentrate on what you are doing?" Even more reasonably, he added: "Unless our friend Bony intends to say something helpful which we ought to hear, although I must say I have been waiting since summer for that to happen."

"But what about the skyboat?" inquired Bess.

"Don't worry about the skyboat. It can fly perfectly well with five oars. For a little while at least." His voice became more urgent. "Go now, boy... and find the way."

So, with a rather forlorn smile of encouragement from Bess, Wake left his position at the back of the skyboat and flew a little way above it and there, all alone, under the glittering silence of the night sky, the stars at last revealed their secret....

It began with the stars starting to fall out of the sky... as he saw what was happening he tried to shout a warning to the others but there was a roaring in his ears from the falling stars and he could not be sure they heard ...a night without stars.. that was certainly strange...

*but he was glad to see they were not disappearing entirely...
they were pouring in glittering drops of light, right down into his
own head... and all the time his mind was widening to contain
them... at last the pouring stopped...*

*now all the stars were in his head but it contained them with
ease because his mind was now as wide as the night itself... all the
stars were there and all in place and he had become the night...*

*...this was certainly more convenient... he no longer had to gaze
around the sky to see the stars... they were all there, inside his
head, and he was actually looking down on them... and because
they were his stars he found he could control them... he reached
down with his thoughts and touched one... and saw with pleasure
that the star he had touched began to grow brighter... another
touch and the star dimmed... he began to feel a little uneasy.. did a
swallow need permission to play with the stars like this?*

*...just at that moment something caught his attention and he
laughed... right in the very centre of his stars a tiny bird had
appeared... the brilliant light was all behind it so that he could not
tell what kind of bird it was but as he watched it started turning...
right in the middle of all his stars the little bird was turning, just
like the rusty iron bird turning in the wind on the roof of the barn...*

*...at the very heart of all those stars, in the still silence of his
mind where there was not a breath of wind to move it, the little bird
was turning round and round, first one way and then another,
searching...*

*and then the little bird's head stopped moving and where he
now pointed a pattern of stars stretching in a ragged line from the
summit of the night right down to the bottom began to fade... all the
other stars were shining just as brightly except for the ones the little
bird had chosen.. they were growing dim...*

*...but there was no time to ponder this mystery for now the stars
were rushing up towards him and in a flash of light so bright that
for a moment he could not see they shot out past his eyes and
hurtled up into the sky again... his mind grew dark... the stars had
gone and so had the little turning bird...*

*feeling vaguely sad he opened his eyes again... everything was
back in place... the eternal ceremony of the stars had resumed but
one thing had changed... as he watched, a pattern of stars
stretching in a ragged line from the summit of the night right down
to the bottom began to grow brighter... they were the stars the little*

turning bird had chosen... using the light they had borrowed from
the stars inside his head they were now clamouring for his attention
with a new and shining insistence.

He closed his eyes in wonder and opened them again, just to be
sure... but they were still there.. a ragged line of stars leading all the
way down the black sky, all the way down to the distant horizon, in
a glittering and unmistakable path.

There, under the stars, Wake laughed and called down to the
others. "There is our path."

Five startled faces looked up at him and it was Bess who spoke.
"What is it? What can you see?" He looked down impatiently. How
could they be so blind?

From the centre of the skyboat came the calm voice of
Creakwing. "They cannot see it and neither can I. They are your
stars. Now if you will be kind enough to set a course we will
proceed to Africa."

This time Wake the swallow leader set a true course for home.
No one else could see the path but this did not matter. All through
the night the skyboat flew on, under his control at last, and all the
time he murmured corrections to their course to keep the skyboat
pointing at that ragged line of stars leading down the sky to the far
horizon and all the time the thought of Africa was growing stronger
in their minds. The revelation of his powers had also affected the
others. Their spirits had lifted; as the skyboat sped along they
chattered excitedly about Africa. There was laughter and teasing
about what they would do when they got there. At one point, Bony
was heard boasting about the possibility of them all being awarded
fame names.[22] Oddly enough none of them asked him any questions
about what had happened while he was away from the skyboat but
now he could see in their eyes a sort of secret respect and Bess in
particular was looking at him in a way we must all hope someone
will one day look at *us*. Creakwing, on the other hand, continued to
regard him with the distaste he reserved for all young swallows and
this was re-assuring in a way.

Something rather curious involving Harold also occurred. Wake

---

[22] *I hope it will not cause too much confusion if I remind you that at that*
time he was obviously not known as Bony !

155

had just made the first correction to keep them aligned with the line of stars when the youngest of the swallows leaned across to Wake from his position on the rear oar and confided in a shy whisper that he thought he could see them, too.

Wake assured him that he was mistaken and hushed him into silence, justifying his response with the argument that one leader was quite enough and that any more would only cause confusion; which only goes to show that even the noblest and bravest among us are quite capable of behaving in ways which are not entirely creditable, once they have taken the precaution of finding a very good reason to do so.

Thinking pleasant thoughts about the many special qualities of leadership and how few swallows ever managed to possess them, Wake continued to guide the skyboat on its southerly course. There was scarcely a breath of wind. The fog had cleared and they had descended to their normal cruising height. Far below the sea was calm. And most wonderful of all, it was growing warmer all the time.

The mood of the travellers grew increasingly carefree. There was a great deal of laughter. At one point the swallows had a long and detailed discussion on a subject they knew nothing about, the possibility that the food in Africa was completely different and even more deliciously plentiful. Creakwing who could easily have resolved the matter merely smiled in a rather dreamy way which suggested that his thoughts had sped on ahead of him and were already there in Africa.

All through the warm night the skyboat flew on, guided by Wake's unseen, starry beacon and when morning came and the stars faded they maintained their course, a little less surely, by the sun. Wake could not help a feeling of apprehension as the sun sank below the horizon that evening but the ragged line of stars was still there, still glittering with that strange intensity. He was intrigued to know how long this would be so; would his stars always shine out so strongly?

"You will see them only twice a year," Creakwing explained. "Once in the spring and again in the autumn. For the rest of the time the stars are the same for everyone."

On the second day after leaving the ship, towards the end of a quiet morning, with the sun directly overhead, there was a sudden explosion of excitement among the swallows. Far to the south, low down and filling the horizon from end to end and shimmering in the midday heat, they saw the land.

"We're there," Bony screamed and immediately he attempted to increase the stroke rate.

"Stop it!" Creakwing bellowed, hanging on desperately and gathering their little store of spare oars under his wings, as the silk of the skyboat stretched tight, threatening to hurl him over the edge.

"You are a fool, boy," Creakwing decreed firmly, once order had been restored. "No doubt about it. But you're not going to change now."

As usual Bony's expression of deep and fervent remorse was an indication of his determination in future to prove that the old leader whom he so admired was mistaken. But as we are about to see he never did change and nobody minded. In the end.

As the day lengthened into afternoon and the shores of Africa came nearer, Wake began to sense that something was troubling Creakwing. At first it had seemed that a great burden had been removed from the old leader as a result of Wake's mysterious experience among the stars. He was visibly more relaxed; seated in the middle of the skyboat, looking around him, enjoying the view from his novel vantage point and even confiding that his wing was feeling a lot better from the effects of the warm sun.

Now, though, his manner had changed. He appeared restless and uneasy. Once he even turned to Wake and suggested that they should try to go a little faster. Only Wake seemed to be aware of this vague disquiet as the skyboat sped on through the warm, still afternoon and then, as though he could no longer hide his anxiety, the old leader turned to him and discreetly directed his attention to the sky behind them. Carefully, so as not to alert the others, Wake followed his gaze and saw that high above them a dark speck had appeared in the sky.

"A little faster, if you please and a little lower," said Creakwing calmly and turning to Wake he added: "If you agree."

"We will land as soon as we reach the shore," said Wake. "It's very hot and it is better if we rest for a while until the sun is lower."

But eventually they were both glancing backwards so frequently that their anxiety could no longer be concealed and the moments passed amid a mounting tension. And all the time the dark shape came nearer until they could see it was a large bird, a bird which was clearly having no difficulty in keeping pace with them. All the swallows were watching it now.

"It is an enemy," said Creakwing. "We must reach the shore. Please hurry."

But the swallows were tiring. This unexpected exertion at the end of the long sea crossing had almost exhausted them. And the dark shape was now directly overhead; circling around the sky in great sweeps, graceful and casual, and gradually sinking lower.

The land was now very close; so near that Wake could see the waves falling on the beach and beyond them a line of sand-dunes. Just to the right of the racing skyboat the dunes were divided by a narrow valley. A little way inland the valley widened out and there on the ground he could see pale shapes like roosting birds and here and there feathers stirring lazily in the breeze from the sea.

"There seem to be some birds on the ground just to the right. We'll be safer with them. Faster now."

Stationary in the yellow sky the dark bird shook with its final, terrible preparations; sharpness was unsheathed, experimentally; desperately the skyboat lunged for the shore. And in that moment Bony surprised them all for the very last time and took his honoured place in the annals of the swallows, alongside those he had always revered.

"Go on," he screamed and there was joy in his cry as he released his oar, soaring above them and turning... now he was flying back the way they had come, out across the sea, away from the skyboat... and the dark bird was following... the steady and monotonous migratory flight of the swallows had gone... Bony was swooping and soaring across the glittering sea, carefree again, flying as once he had flown above the pond... away he went, back towards the north, dancing across the sky as though he had not a care in the world... rising to greet his destiny... the dark bird followed, away from the skyboat.. it seemed puzzled by the strangeness of the moment... and then it remembered its hunger... devoid of thought, it dived... and the sky behind the swallows was empty again.

With a choked sob Oliver attempted to turn to keep the sky in view where Bony had vanished and as he did so the oar slipped from his beak. With both front oars now unattended the skyboat was unstable and disaster came quickly. A breeze snatched the front edge sending it billowing backwards, enveloping Creakwing and wrapping itself around Winnie's central oar, so that every sweep of her wings snagged against the material. The oar dropped from her beak. Only three oars were now functioning and the skyboat began to fall. The little store of reserve oars went cascading downwards as Creakwing struggled to escape from the folds of silk. But at least they were now over the land. "The valley," screamed Wake. "Make for the valley."

With only three of them now flying the skyboat they could feel the oars tearing at their beaks as the weight of the foundering craft bore them down. Both Oliver and Winnie were fluttering alongside desperately trying to recover their oars, but it was hopeless. They were falling even faster. Wake, clinging on with Harold at the rear, became aware of Bess still in position at the central oar in front of him. She, at least, could be saved. "Let go. It's no use. Let go and save yourself." But Creakwing was still trapped; Bess shook her head grimly and hung on. And a few seconds later it was all over.

One side of the valley was an almost sheer slope with an enormous ledge of rock jutting out near the top. With no one controlling it, this was where the skyboat struck, snapping three of the oars and tearing open the holes where they were attached to the material. Stunned by the impact the swallows were unable to recover quickly enough. The skyboat rolled helplessly to the edge of the rocky ledge and then fell in a tangled and fluttering confusion down to the valley floor. There was a single piercing cry from Bess and then a great silence.

At first the silence was such a pleasant change that Wake was not too worried to discover that he was lying quite still with his face in the hot sand. Unable to recall how he got there, he decided instead to concentrate on the important task of trying to raise his head and after a great deal of groaning which he listened to with interest he did so and looked around him.

How silly, he thought. They were not birds he had seen from the sky; they were bones. Everywhere he looked he could see the pale gleam of bones. They were the bones of birds. Some were clearly of ancient origin but to some there were feathers still clinging and as he gazed around him a little breeze crept along the hot and shimmering surface of the valley floor and the feathers stirred playfully, so that he thought to himself how pretty they looked.

The swallows were lying almost under the ledge of rock. It was now late in the afternoon and already the shadows were starting to spread across the valley floor. For the first time since the Crossing had begun he felt deliciously sleepy and free from anxiety. He wondered if the others were finding it equally pleasant to be resting in such a quiet place after all those days spent flying over the stormy sea.

A name came into his mind; the name was Bess and so he said it out loud and one of the swallows lying beside him lifted her head and tried to smile and then lowered it again. One of the other swallows whose name he could not quite remember seemed to be weeping.

"He did it to save us. He knew what was going to happen and he did it for us."

He waited for a moment to see if she would say something else to make things clearer but she just continued sobbing quietly, so he turned his attention to the wreckage lying all around them. The skyboat also seemed perfectly content to be lying there in the soft, hot sand, its long journey finally over.

So that was that. He had not known until that moment how strong was his craving for rest; how weary he was of endless travelling and the ceaseless motion of the sea; weary of constant change; and above all, weary of the need for thought. Here there was no movement, no thought; only the heat and the silence, closing protectively around them, as the desert made them welcome. He gazed out across the valley and watched the bones breathing gently in the burning heat. Why should they not stay here, for ever?

His eyes closed. He seemed to open them again immediately but in that short time night had fallen. It was bitterly cold and he was shivering violently. The night was clear and he looked up and saw that a ragged line of stars brighter than all the rest still ran down the sky but now they touched a range of hills far away to the south. He gazed up at them in gratitude. It wasn't your fault, he told them; you were not to blame.

And then he fell asleep and soon all the swallows were sleeping, so quiet and so still that it was impossible to distinguish them from the silent companions sleeping all around them in the dark.

Soon, the desert whispered to itself, very soon...

* * *

In The Valley Of Bones

He entered the valley just after dawn. The donkey he was riding was old and also very tired. They had been travelling all through the night to reach this remote place and as they entered the valley the donkey felt an old and familiar dread and began to pick his way nervously through the ancient litter of bones. The boy sensed the donkey's fear and stroked the rough and matted skin of his neck with long, fine fingers.

"Do not be afraid. It is the last time. And then we can go home."

A long and stony slope led down into the valley from the south and when he was a little way down it the boy stopped; from there he could see the whole length of it stretching away from him to where the sea glittered in the early morning sun. He could sense the growing perturbation of the donkey beneath him and asked himself if it was really necessary this time to go any further. In front of him nothing moved in the valley apart from the places where the early morning breeze was stirring the feathers of the birds which had died there. The boy averted his gaze from this sight and several minutes went by, as he gazed blankly down the slope enjoying the feel of the returning sun on his face and thinking about food.

It had taken him two days to reach the valley. So far as he knew it was a place known only to him because even though his people were wanderers of the desert it lay far away from any of the paths which they might take. Nor had he ever discussed it with them; especially not with the other boys.

As usual they had gathered around to watch his simple preparations for departure. And as usual, as he loaded the donkey, one or other of them had sought to enliven the proceedings by suddenly starting to rush around in circles flapping his arms and squawking, but this was now a very old joke and even they were growing rather tired of it.

To be truthful they were also growing rather bored with him; bored with his slow deliberate movements and his failure to respond when they taunted him. They were always quite relieved when he was finally mounted on his donkey and plodding away from the encampment on yet another of his mysterious wanderings. At first the old men had railed against these absences, accusing him of neglecting his duties, but they did so with gentle exasperation because they knew that when there was work to be done no one worked harder than the boy; he would even seek out things to do, to atone for the days when he was not there.

For all of his sixteen years the boy had wandered with his people across the vast and empty spaces of the desert and in that time, because he had no family of his own, his spirit had also wandered unencumbered through the spaces of the heart. That was how he had come to admire the birds, because they, too, were wanderers. While still very young he had looked up and watched the sky grow dark with them at certain times of the year, wondering where they came from and where they were going. Watching the birds passing overhead in such vast numbers he had come to believe that somewhere there must be places where they had to land to rest and recover, either from the desert or the sea. And eventually he had found the valley.

The first time he saw it he was afraid. He had expected the resting place of the birds to be a place of life, filled with noise and movement, but the valley lay precisely at the end of the two great ordeals of the sea and the sands and for that reason had been for countless ages a place of exhaustion, despair and death. It was a place which had always filled the boy with dread because it seemed as though there was something in the valley itself which led the birds down to their doom.

It was such an awful place that he would never have returned had it not been for something which happened that very first time; there, in the valley of bones, he had come upon life; the warm and wildly quivering form of a tiny bird lying alone amid all that ghastly display, exhausted and close to death. Gently and patiently the boy had persuaded the little bird to drink a few drops of water and eat a little food and after a short time he had watched it flutter from his hand and resume its journey to the south. Since then there had been others and now with the autumn migration long over the boy was making his last visit to the valley, just in case, although he did not really expect to find any signs of life so late in the year.

The boy was both hungry and tired after travelling through the night but he had no intention of eating or resting until he had left that place of death, so he pulled gently on the reins to return up the slope, allowing his gaze to sweep the valley for one last time. And that was when he saw it; a flash of colour, far away to the seaward end of the valley. He had not noticed it at first because his eyes had been searching for movement, not colour. To a desert dweller like the boy any bright colour was a novel experience and as he gazed at this sight, so unexpected amid the drabness of the sand, it seemed to him that the flash of yellow was actually signalling its presence. His knees tightened against the donkey's flanks and he felt it stiffen in resistance to his will. The delay had made it believe that this time it would not have to face the ordeal of the valley and now it was afraid again. The boy had to lean forward and whisper to the donkey before it would consent to start moving reluctantly down the slope. Dust rose around them as they moved across the valley towards the place where the boy had seen the flash of colour and even though the donkey moved now with nervous caution from time to time brittle things crunched and broke under its tentative hooves.

Several times the donkey stopped altogether and gazed forlornly back at him but although the boy was now strangely excited at the prospect of what he might find he betrayed no impatience with these hesitations. He merely waited, gently stroking that rough neck, until the donkey's hooves found a new way through that pallid litter. Even after so many visits to the valley he, too, was always anxious to leave a place where it seemed that the spirit of death itself was present and gloating over its ghastly hoard.

When they reached the place the boy pulled gently on the reins and as the dust stirred up by their approach settled slowly down around them he rummaged among his faded rags and took out his most important possession. The spectacle case was now so old that most of the fabric had worn away to reveal the silvery glint of metal underneath but the glasses inside the case were unmarked by the passage of time.

The glasses had changed the boy's life. If he had been like the rest of his people his eyes would have served him well because he could see clearly for vast distances across the desert but he wanted only to see the detail of things and in this his eyes had failed him. One day while he was trying to examine an object he had picked up out in the desert one of the old women watched him grimacing as he held it close to his face. She went to the large suitcase in which her own life was now all stored away and rummaged around until she found an old pair of glasses. In the days when he was young her husband had visited the great city on the coast to purchase the glasses. Now she wished the boy to have them. They were half-glasses and they hung down on the boy's nose so that he looked like a wise old man. The old woman who had not laughed for a long time laughed out loud when she saw the boy wearing her dead husband's glasses and so did the other boys. They gave him the name of Kamar Wagh (moon-face) but he did not care because at last he could see clearly.

These were the glasses he now put on. During all the years he had explored the desert he had seen many things for which he had been able to find no explanation; nor had there been anyone to talk to about these matters. To his wild nature it now seemed that all things were possible so he gazed down not with wonder but with curiosity at the sight which he now saw clearly for the first time.

The object which had attracted his attention from the top of the valley was a square of orange silk, with a bright yellow sun in the centre. The colours had faded and the material was badly torn. And clustered around it on the sand, exhausted and frightened, there were six tiny birds.

Still seated on the back of the donkey the boy studied the birds in silence and then a curious sound began to issue from his throat; it was a thin, high, consoling sound. The donkey had heard it several times before but it was still so strange that it stirred uneasily beneath him. Again he reached down and allowed his hand to rest on that rough skin, as the delicate sound continued. The boy waited until he saw the fierce light fading from the eyes regarding him from the ground and then he rose up in the saddle and slowly and carefully dismounted.

The stricken birds did not stir as he approached. Continuing to soothe them with that eerie sound, only more softly now, with his scholarly spectacles resting on the end of his nose, he began to examine them one by one. Tiny hearts pounded madly against his fingers but they did not resist. Four of the birds, though thin and unkempt, seemed to be uninjured. One of them had a leg bent to one side and clearly broken. The largest of them appeared to be suffering from an old injury. Just where the wing joined the body two small lumps were visible under the skin. They were round and hard to the touch and because they were lodged in a sinew of muscle it was impossible for the bird fully to open the wing. It was not the first time the boy had seen such an injury.

"Someone has been trying to kill you, little bird."

Satisfied that the birds were now calm the boy began his preparations. He went to the donkey and removed his water pouch and hung it over his shoulder and then he released the straps of one of the two panniers slung across the donkey's back and removed a folded cloth. Returning to the birds he knelt down beside them and from a pocket in his robes took out a tiny, silver thimble. He filled it to the brim with water and then he moved from bird to bird allowing them to drink their fill. They drank eagerly, their eyes glittering watchfully above the rim of the little cup, and several times it was necessary to replenish the thimble from the water bottle.

When he saw that they could drink no more the boy cleared a space beside them and spread the cloth open on the sand. His eyes checked the contents, establishing that everything he needed was there and then he flung off his robe to reveal a ragged shirt and trousers and reached down for the bird with the broken leg. It was just as his fingers were about to close around it that the bird lying next to it reacted. Without warning it pecked at his hand, so sharply that a little spot of blood appeared. The boy sucked the wound ruefully.

"It's all right, little warrior. I mean her no harm."

Their eyes met for a moment and this time when he reached down there was no hostility from the little bird's protector. The boy worked without hesitation, the movements of his long brown fingers swift and bold. Behind his scholarly spectacles his eyes betrayed no anxiety. And all the time a gentle clucking sound soothed the little frightened bird. Carefully he felt for the ends of the broken bone under the skin, his face calm and expressionless, as his mind tried to picture what his eyes could not see. When he was satisfied that the picture in his mind was complete he fitted the two ends together, so tenderly that the injured bird scarcely stirred. Next he picked up a bundle of tiny splints made from peeled slivers of green bark, selected one, and bound it tightly to the leg he had just set, with a thin cotton thread. Only then did his face relax into a smile.

"That should last until your leg is strong again," he said. He turned his gaze on the bird which had attacked him. "I hope you are no longer angry with me, little warrior."

The boy now picked up the bird with the wing which would not open. With his left hand enclosing it so that only its head was visible he began to stare steadily into the eyes of the injured bird, as the fingers of his other hand searched through the contents of the cloth, finally closing around a small knife. With his gaze still fixed on the bird he opened the knife by touch alone and tested the blade against his finger. Cautiously he adjusted his grip on the injured bird and then allowed his fingers to part, revealing that the two round lumps now lay between them. He stretched the flesh under his hand to emphasise their shape. The little bird continued to hold his gaze as though in a trance.

"It is necessary," the boy murmured. And raised the knife.

He parted the flesh of the little bird with two crossed cuts, just where one of the lumps now strained against the skin and as the incision appeared he squeezed and a small crimson pellet of lead popped out into his hand. The little bird shuddered beneath his fingers. Screened by his hand from the reality of what was happening the birds on the ground watched uncomprehendingly. "It is almost over," he whispered. And again he took the blade to the stretched skin and a second piece of shot was forced out between his fingers.

Holding the sides of the first wound together with his fingers he smeared the cut with ointment from a little pot and repeated the action with the second and then he waited, occasionally testing the surface with the tip of his finger. The sun was now directly overhead and the dressing quickly hardened in the hot, dry air.

All this time the little bird's companions had been watching him warily from the ground and now he held it up for them to see. Very gently he opened and closed the wing, demonstrating that it could move freely once more without discomfort. As he examined the flat, smooth surface where he had removed the lumps of shot, just for a moment behind the old man's glasses, the boy's eyes betrayed an exultant joy. It was as though he had prevailed against an enemy; he felt an impulse to shout his triumph to the valley but instead he reached down and replaced the little bird on the ground beside its companions.

"And remember not to touch," he instructed gravely and turned his attention to the coloured handkerchief which had first attracted his attention. Examining it more closely he saw features he had not noticed before. There was a line of precisely spaced holes running down each side of the handkerchief, some of them obviously torn open by the impact with the ground. Hooked through several of them were short lengths of twig. These had clearly snapped in two because the matching sections were lying around on the sand. Only one of the twigs remained undamaged and still hooked through the material. For some time the boy continued to gaze down at the handkerchief. Until that moment he had been unable to understand how the largest of the birds had found it possible to fly at all with a crippled wing, let alone to reach this remote place; now he understood.

"So this was a rescue attempt," he murmured.

He gazed back in the direction from which he had come. Far to the south the mountains appeared very close in the clear and cloudless air and high above them he could see large birds slowly circling. Down at his feet the little birds from the north watched him with no apparent fear. In the valley itself, for as far as he could see, nothing moved, except where the plumes of the fallen faintly stirred in the wind from the sea, as though this was an ancient field of honour where great deeds had been done. Standing there alone in that place of death the boy could sense the presence of his adversary.

Again he studied the ragged handkerchief and the exhausted little birds sprawled in the sand around it. He knew nothing of their home in the far north, only that every year it grew so dark and cold there that many birds could no longer survive and were forced to set off on their long and arduous journey; a journey which had so often ended here. Some of them probably perished in the valley without ever knowing how near they had been to their southern home, for just beyond those distant mountains lay the land they were seeking. It was as he gazed south towards the mountains and the great birds ceaselessly soaring and swooping above them, on the rising currents of air, that the idea was born in the mind of the boy. And he said out loud to the valley: "These at least you will not have."

It was now early in the afternoon and for the remainder of the day the boy was very busy. From the folded cloth he took out the needle and thread he had often used to sew up the wounds of the birds he had found and began carefully to repair the tears in the sides of the handkerchief. Next he abandoned the shade at the side of the valley and walked out into the sun.

The heat was so intense that it lay like a molten pool in the bowl of the valley, resisting his progress and closing behind him with every step he took. Despite his discomfort he wandered about the valley for some time selecting objects from the ground and placing them in the cloth. At last with the sun sinking lower in the sky he returned to the birds which were lying exactly as he had left them. From the cloth he took a flat length of wood, smooth and familiar, and placed it in the bottom of one of the donkey's panniers, to create a wide deep recess and then he placed the cloth in the bottom. On top of it he carefully laid the coloured handkerchief; and again his throat began to produce that strange, inhuman sound, as one by one, feeling their fear quivering through his fingers, he picked up the tiny birds and placed them down, right in the middle of the handkerchief, on the faded yellow sun in the centre of the faded sky, reserving a special tenderness for the two he knew to be in pain. Then he climbed back on the donkey.

"It is over. We are leaving."

All day the donkey had waited in patient anxiety for the signal to leave and when the boy finally urged him forward he responded at once. They headed south, towards the mountains. The boy was excited and once or twice he clucked his tongue impatiently and pressed his knees into the donkey's sides; the donkey ignored him. Now that they were moving again all authority was invested in the unalterable rhythm of those slow and plodding steps and the boy gave a little shrug and smiled to himself in the darkness at the thought of it.

Even if they could not go any faster he did not intend to stop. He knew how urgent their journey had become; for the little birds, exhausted and thin with a hunger he could not satisfy, there was not much time remaining. As the sun sank lower and a cold and steady wind began to blow across the desert he re-arranged the complicated pattern of his robes more effectively around him and hunched lower in the saddle..

Morning revealed the boy and the donkey still plodding south across the empty sands until at last in the middle of the day the hot weight of the sun was too much to bear and the boy spread his robe over the dry branches of a desert shrub and for a few hours they rested in its shade.

All through the following night they continued their journey south and the boy kept his spirits high by glancing upwards from time to time to see how the deeper darkness of the hills was coming nearer all the time. Eventually he felt the donkey's steps becoming more laboured and knew that they had embarked upon the upward slope. Soon afterwards he dismounted and began moving forward on foot leading the donkey by the reins. From time to time he would peer down into the pannier and see the glitter of watchful eyes.

Eventually, in the darkest part of the night, it became too hazardous for them to continue; the uneven surface and the steepness of the slope meant that they were stumbling at almost every step, so the boy tugged on the reins and pulled the donkey down into a stony hollow where the wind could not reach them. There, pressed into the wide, warm back of the donkey, with his robes tightly drawn around him, he dozed away the hours until dawn.

As the light returned he was able to see that their steps had been leading them up towards a high ridge between two rocky peaks. The slope they had still to traverse rose sharply up towards the ridge, trackless and strewn with the debris of massive boulders dislodged from above. It was towards this discouraging prospect that the boy now directed the donkey's steps.

All morning they toiled upwards. The donkey had spent all its life on the flat desert sands and found the journey up towards the empty sky strange and inexplicable. Sometimes it lost its footing and scrambled desperately to retain a hold on the loose surface. The stones would then scuttle away down the slope behind them as the frantic braying of the donkey resounded between the rocky walls now enclosing them in shadow on either side.

The boy scarcely noticed the difficulties. His eyes constantly scanned the sky above the summit of the ridge and eventually towards the middle of the morning he saw what he had been waiting for. High above the peak to their left a number of large birds had appeared in the sky and were circling lazily close to the summit. The growing strength of the sun was heating the air and causing it to rise and as they sensed the unseen force beneath them the birds would open their enormous wings and allow the rising columns of air to bear them swiftly upwards.

The boy observed this with satisfaction and as they struggled on towards the ridge he kept looking up towards the high ceremony of the endlessly circling birds, just to re-assure himself that everything was happening as he had planned. Once he reached down into the pannier in front of him where the little birds had lain ever since the journey began and his fingers caressed them gently.

"Today," he murmured, "you will be going home."

It was almost the middle of the day when they finally came to the crest of the ridge and there the boy stood, supporting his head and arms on the compliant back of the donkey, listening to the beat of his heart growing steadily calmer after the exertion of the long climb and gazing out to the south. Now it was clear why no tracks led to this place. Here at the top of the ridge the ground in front fell away much more steeply than on the side they had approached it from. Only the most intrepid of travellers would have dared to descend this precipitous gradient falling away to the desert floor, lying empty and silent in the glare of the sun far below.

But it was not the prospect immediately below which interested him; his eyes were straining into the haze far away to the south and as he did so a little smile crossed his features and he softly patted the donkey's back in gratitude. Almost at the limits of the horizon, trembling in the heat, he could see at last the beginnings of green. He dismounted and tethered the donkey a few steps back from the edge of the abyss by laying the reins on a ledge of rock and weighing them down with a large stone and then he took the orange square of silk out of the pannier, with the little birds still inside it, and laid it down on the stony ground in front of him.

This time the soothing sounds were not necessary. As he lifted them out one by one from the folds of silk and placed them on the ground their eyes showed no fear, nor did they stir as the boy began his final preparations. He opened the folded piece of cloth and removed the objects he had selected from the valley floor. Even though they had been the longest and thickest feathers he could find he examined them again, selecting the two which were perfect for his purpose. When he was satisfied he took out his knife. He laid each of the feathers in turn across a large flat stone and cut through it at the point where it began to taper away into soft and downy vanes and then he trimmed it at one end into a strong, sharp point, testing it with his finger.

Even with his robes laid aside the boy was perspiring. He sank back on his heels and wiped his streaming brow with a corner of the garment. With his hand shielding his eyes from the full glare of the burning sky he re-assured himself that the birds were still there, circling close to the summit, rising and falling on those invisible fountains of air and then he turned his attention to the piece of silk. He used his knife to make four new cuts near each corner, taking care to avoid the neat lines of stitches were he had repaired the material. All the time he was aware of the six little birds watching his movements almost as though they understood what he was doing.

"Now you will see," he said and he took one of the feathers and threaded it down through one of the holes in the corner of the silk square, under the material and up through the hole on the other side. Because he had inserted the feather against the flow of the vanes it was much more firmly held. He repeated the process with the second feather and laid the handkerchief down on the ground in front of him. As he had calculated, even after being trimmed the feathers were still long enough to extend outwards like oars from the edge of the material on each side but in order to increase the clearance still further he gathered the silk in a little towards the centre.

He was well-pleased with his efforts and because he thought it desirable now to show someone what he had achieved he called out to the donkey who after deep consideration slowly turned his head and gazed back at him with dismal indifference. The boy held up the contraption of silk and feathers.

"Behold, oh miserable one. It is finished. And now we can all go home."

He moved to the brink of the abyss and spread the square of silk out on the ground, adjusting the feathers so that they extended precisely at right angles from the edges of the material. Picking up one of the little birds he placed it in position beside one of the oars and repeated the process until there was one of the uninjured birds stationed at each of the four corners. Next he reached out for the bird with the broken leg, saying: "For you, there will be a magic carpet. Just like Sinbad." And he placed it down in the centre of the silk square on top of the faded yellow sun. That left only the bird he had operated on. The boy picked it up and examined the wounds for the last time, touching the dried ointment with the tip of his finger.

"You will not be carrying anything," he said. "Just in case." Once more the boy sank back on his heels and as he gazed down at the little birds he felt sad with the imminence of parting. "You have travelled far from your winter home and one of you, I think, has been lost along the way. But it is almost over."

The eyes which glittered up at the boy from the ground were filled with cold indifference. He felt suddenly tired. He closed his eyes, his mind empty of thought..

And then it was as though he began to remember things, except that they were things he had never known and he was seeing them from above, like a bird...

He saw water, reed-fringed and stirred by the wind... a blue sky above with soft white clouds.. he watched a wide river flowing between great banks of sand... there was an old red wall slumbering in the sun... a dim interior alive with the twittering excitement of tiny birds.. just for a moment the boy shivered in the presence of snow and then he was high above the sea and travelling towards the sun.. a dark speck appeared in the sky far away behind him and the boy felt fear... and then darkness struck him like a blow and the voices began....

You must go on now.
But why did we ever leave ?
We left to live and now you who are left must go on.
We were happy there.
You will be happy again but now you must go on.
Why must we go on? We are weary of travelling.
If you stay here now I will be forgotten.
We will never forget you.
If you die here there will be no one left to remember
And I will have no fame.
How much farther?
From here you can see the place.
How will we know it?
There will be green, at last.
We are too tired.
It does not matter. See the birds above the mountains? How they rise on the air? You will do the same.
Come with us.
I will be there.

As the birds moved out across the abyss, for a strange moment it seemed to the boy that for a little while at least he was flying with them and then they were flying faster and he was being left behind. Almost at once they appeared to be in difficulty; the fluttering silk began to sink; just for a moment he ceased to breathe. And then like an unseen hand the warm and solicitous air reached up towards them. The little birds opened their wings joyfully and the square of silk began to rise again, higher and higher into the sky above him.

Now, in the wind, the feathers taken from the valley seemed to be alive again, and because his eyes were blurred by tears it seemed to the boy that a large and ghostly bird was carrying the little birds away from him. Standing there at the edge of the cliff he continued to watch the southern sky until the little birds faded from his sight and for a long time afterwards as he and the donkey retraced their steps down from the ridge they travelled on through his mind.

* * *

That was how the swallows finally came home, with some degree of ceremony, flying in down an endless avenue of airy fountains, leaping and soaring beneath them.

Wake and Harold were on the front oars with Winnie and Oliver behind. In the centre of the handkerchief the injured Bess had taken the place of Creakwing who was enormously insistent that his proper place was flying at the rear. No one, especially not Wake, disagreed with this opinion. With only four of them supporting the weight of the injured Bess there is no doubt that they would gradually have sunk to the desert floor had it not been for the assistance of the thermals and if that had happened it is probable that they would never have been heard of again. But each time they felt they had lost too much height the four swallows flying the skyboat would simply open their wings and soar upwards again on the rising columns of warmer air, just like the great birds circling the peaks of the mountains now lying to the north of them.

In this way the swallows flew on southwards over the desert for the remainder of the day and as the sun sank lower in the sky Wake allowed the currents of air to lift them so high that it took all night for them to descend. Navigation, of course, was not a problem. Despite the interruption occasioned by their crash landing Wake's starry path had appeared precisely as before and continued to guide them for the remainder of the journey.

As dawn broke the following day the swallows saw a sight they had often thought they would never see again. Once more they were flying over land which was green; though not half so green as the land they had left so far to the north. Here and there they could also see the gleam of water. From far below, astonishingly loud and clear in the still morning air, came the familiar excitement of the dawn chorus. And as he heard it Wake fervently vowed that he would never complain about it ever again.

Soon afterwards the first feeding swallows of the day rose into the sky and discovered them. "We knew you were coming," they cried, mystifyingly. They were unknown to Wake and his companions but they quickly moved in alongside the skyboat, attempting to share their burden. The newcomers, of course, knew nothing about the technique of flying the skyboat and with so many extra assistants grasping the feathered oars their slow and elegant descent rapidly changed into a wild and wobbling climb back towards the upper air, as though Wake and his companions had been refused permission to land and were being ushered away! In the end he had to speak very sternly to the newcomers and warn them to leave the oars alone. All this time younger and less serious swallows had been swooping and soaring all over the sky and forgetting breakfast in their wild excitement.

They flew on, in this ceremonial way, for a little while longer until the moment when the swallows finally realised they had reached their own little part of the enormous land called Africa. They knew they had arrived because all at once the skyboat was gliding in above a landscape strangely like the one which they had left; they saw a river and farm buildings and a pond fringed with reeds and trees; there was even a long wire fence crowded from end to end with waiting swallows. For a moment they had the oddest feeling that they had travelled in a vast circle and returned to the place they had left, except that this place was warm and sunny with not a trace of winter. Creakwing who was thoroughly enjoying the sensation caused by their arrival explained.

"It is a tradition of the swallows. We like our summer and winter homes to appear to be the same, like reflections in the water, so that wherever we happen to be, we always feel at home. Very important, I assure you, for those swallows who have to do a great deal of travelling back and forth." He smiled benignly. "As you will have to do."

After the first excitement of their arrival and the endless questions one or two of the more perceptive and sensitive swallows began to drift away. As they did so they signalled discreetly to others in an attempt to persuade them to leave and if this failed to do the trick they stood beside them and shoved. Soon only the least sensitive swallows were still there, insisting on answers to their questions and they had to be forcibly removed. At last the five youngest swallows were alone with their mothers. We shall also steal away at this point, although there is one thing about this private re-union you should know; immediately after it had taken place all the mothers went to sit with Bony's mother and actually spent rather more time with her than they had spent with their own long-lost offspring.

Safe now in their winter home the swallows grew fatter and

stronger every day. After a few weeks the splint was removed from Bess's leg and she was able to use it again exactly as before. Creakwing's [23] wounds also healed. He found that now he could fly as well as ever. But there in their winter home food was plentiful and the sun was warm and constant. Several other old swallows who had decided to spend their retirement in the south were there to keep him company and one morning he officially announced that he had no intention ever again of making the long and tedious journey north to their summer home.

"I always preferred this place anyway," he confided to his cronies. "Summer up there was always too much like winter for my liking." And he added that anyway he had rather lost interest in the mating season.

In that connection there is another matter I must bring to your attention. I know such mushy matters are deeply distasteful to many of you and I give you my word that there will be no further reference to it. During the ordeal of the Winter Crossing a deep bond of respect and affection had developed between Wake and Bess and when they eventually returned to their summer home let us say that they were more than just good friends. In fact in years to come whenever they fulfilled an engagement to lecture on the Winter Crossing it was more likely than not that the audience would include their own delightful offspring, bestowing on their parents the sort of rapt and respectful attention few of us are ever able to command from our own children.

The winter the swallows had so spectacularly escaped from turned out to be one of the worst there had ever been. All the resident birds struggled for food and shelter; many grew weak and died. The winter went on for so long that the birds who were enduring it began to believe that this time perhaps it intended to stay for ever. But what can resist April? One morning towards the middle of that month, the world awoke to a wonderful new light and a warm and kindly wind, blowing in across the estuary, stroking every living thing. Fluffy young clouds were dashing about in a wide, blue sky, under the gaze of an amiable sun. The watery, windy sounds of the pond had returned. High up in the tops of the

---

[23] *As with many human nicknames the explanation for this one gradually came to be forgotten but the swallows just went on using it*

swaying, rustling trees, with fresh and forgetful hope, the rooks were building again. And no matter where you went around the estuary it seemed that far away you could hear the sound of children laughing.

On that perfect morning the old man who had spent all winter indoors, looked out of the window and said to himself, very firmly: "That's it then. I've had enough of this. I'm going outside." As was his custom he took his old armchair out on to the grass behind the farmhouse, for a little snooze. And awoke to a considerable surprise!

All through the winter, off and on, he had been wondering about his old handkerchief, loudly speculating about where it could have gone and bitterly accusing anyone who could not offer a satisfactory explanation as to where they were when it disappeared. Since he was not entirely clear precisely when this was everyone in the house had fallen under suspicion. Who, he would loudly complain, would steal an old man's fine and only silk handkerchief? At times he made such a nuisance of himself that his daughter grew thoroughly exasperated and said: "For Heaven's sake, Dad. Stop going on about it. It'll turn up."

What he had not expected was that it would turn up outside, for when he awoke there it was, hanging from a branch of a tree at the bottom of the garden, even though he was convinced it had not been there when he closed his eyes. Sorely puzzled, the old man walked slowly down the garden and stood for a moment under the blossom-laden apple tree. And then he reached up and removed the handkerchief and examined it in amazement.

The handkerchief now looked quite different. The vivid colours of the sky and the sun were faded and drab; it was tattered at the edges. There was a small tear in the middle and four neat holes had appeared in each of the four corners. Most astonishing of all, there were several places where the handkerchief appeared to have been torn and then sewn together again.

"Well, I'm blowed," the old man said .Then, because he was also an old soldier, he added: "It looks like a flag that's been carried in a war. Where on earth has it been, though, and how did it get back here?"

He was so amazed and delighted to see his old handkerchief again, even in its damaged condition, that he decided to go inside and find someone to astonish with the story of the way it had been returned to him. First, though, he gazed suspiciously all around the sunlit garden just to be sure that whoever had returned the handkerchief was not still there. He was quite relieved to see that he was still alone.

But of course, in coming to this conclusion, he did not take into account the birds... the blue tit actually sitting in that very apple tree... the three jackdaws perched in a tree at the bottom of the garden... or the swallows, just five of them, circling low above the garden in the warm breezes of that first lovely, April morning. Nor did he notice that for some unaccountable reason the little yellow bird in his cage in front of the open window was singing so loudly and with such utter and complete delight that you might have supposed they could hear his song as far away as Africa.

The End

Printed in the United Kingdom
by Lightning Source UK Ltd.
104287UKS00001B/220-243